I0596176

THE VISITOR

A NOVEL

J. R. Klein

Publisher: Del Gato
Second Edition
Cover Image: Ruslan Moore
Library of Congress Control Number: 2020905048
ISBN: 978-1-7339069-6-8
ISBN: 978-1-733-9069-7-5 (ebook)

For Jeanne

ACKNOWLEDGMENTS

First and foremost, I wish to thank my wife Jeanne for her countless insights into many aspects of the novel. I also thank my sister Mary Beth and her husband Rich, along with their son Aaron and his wife Teresa, and their daughter Amy and her husband Tom, from whom I learned to speak Minnesotan…a little bit. Finally, I am grateful to have spent time in Winona, Minnesota, where I gained a sense of life in a small town like Cedar Bluff.

1

Ben Malone is not a nosey person, not someone who pokes around in other people's business. Why would he? He has his own problems, his own headaches, his own fish to fry. He's your basic go along to get along sort of guy—que sera sera. So, it's fine with him that Victor Cartuso moves in next door, someone who is nice, pleasant, friendly…normal.

In a town like Cedar Bluff, you can't get away with much. Two-thousand four hundred and thirty-six people give or take what happens at Memorial Hospital during the night.

But Ben didn't grow up in the Bluff, Amy did. Ben is from Chicago, and in a place that big, your next-door neighbor could be manufacturing counterfeit bills in the basement, could be a serial killer, may well be posting lewd pictures of himself—or herself—on the internet. You'd never know. But in the Bluff you can't get away with diddly. That's what people like to believe.

The first day Victor Cartuso moves in, Amy pops over with an apple pie for their new neighbor. Not a cherry pie, or a peach pie, or coconut cream (Ben's favorite), but a homemade apple pie.

"Oh ye-uh, let me tell you, seems real nice," Amy says when she returns.

"That's good," Ben replies. But then everyone in the Bluff is real nice, even those who just arrived—if you buy into the hype about the place. Well, Ben doesn't buy into it, not all of it, anyway. How often has he told Amy, "Try doing what I do every day. Try being nice to every Tom, Bill, and Sally that comes into your Shell station. The ones who buzz in late for work with an empty gas tank and it's all *Ben's* fault, of course. Or the ones who think he's over-charging for the Twinkies and Ho-Hos and Beef Jerky compared to the Safeway. Fine, buy your freaking Twinkies and Ho-Hos and Jerky at the Safeway. Just once, Ben would love to say, "In case they haven't noticed, I'm not in the Twinkie and Ho-Ho business. I sell gas and tires, replace brake pads, do tune-ups." But he smiles and sucks it up.

"He's a writer," Amy says. "Mystery novels."

"Mystery novels, huh? What's his name?"

"Victor…Victor Cartuso."

"Writer, huh?"

"That's what he said. He came from out east. He thinks he can work better here with fewer distractions."

"Well, if he wants quiet, he'll get it in the Bluff," Ben says, wrestling with a page of the newspaper. "Yeup, we have *lots* of quiet in the Bluff…lots."

Amy calls upstairs to Jimmy. We'll be eating soon she tells him.

Ben sets the paper down and gives Amy a curious look. "Why would he come here? Hardly anyone moves into the Bluff. Wonder how he found out about it?"

"Oh, who knows, heard about it from friends maybe. Or relatives. You know, hon, this *isn't* the end of the earth…"

"Pert near," Ben says.

Amy turns a frown on him. "Well…in spite of what you sometimes think, it's not."

And she's right. He does sometimes think Cedar Bluff is the end of the earth. It's been almost ten years since they moved in and Ben hasn't fully adjusted—probably never will. But Amy was convinced it would be good for Jimmy.

Back then Amy's parents lived just across town. In Cedar Bluff just across town means barely two miles. Her parents are gone now but Ben and Amy stayed. And the Shell station is doing fine. And the house is paid for. And they'd never be able to afford much in the big city these days. For what you pay to live in Cedar Bluff, you could barely afford a basement flat in Berwyn or Cicero or Brookfield on the west side of Chicago, let alone a nice spot on the north side, or in a hoity-toity neighborhood like La Grange or Hinsdale or Oak Brook, let's say.

Ben taps his fingers on the table. "Maybe we should run a criminal background check."

Amy pulls a pan off the stove and looks harshly at him. "Oh Ben, *please*!"

"Just kidding." Yet, more than once, Ben's made the claim that small towns make people suspicious. He says he'd never even suggest such a thing in Chicago, never even think it. But when you know everything that's going on around you—or you think you do—you start wondering about everyone's motives.

"I'm sure he's a fine person," Amy says. "And think how great it is for Jimmy. He can say he's living next to a writer, an actual writer. Oh, now imagine that! What are the chances of *that* here in the Bluff?"

"Ah ye-uh, and pretty soon every fucking hayseed coming into the Shell will be saying, 'Sooo…what's that writer fella next to you doing these days, Ben?' You can't keep a secret from anyone in this town."

"You shouldn't do that, drop the F-bomb with Jimmy around."

"Are you kidding? Have you heard him when he thinks we're not listening?"

"Doesn't matter, no point in encouraging him."

Ben sets the table. Jimmy comes down and takes his place.

"Did you meet the new neighbor?" Amy asks Jimmy.

"Talked to him," Jimmy replies, indifferently.

"Oh, you don't say. When?"

"This afternoon."

"What did he say?"

"Said he has a son about my age."

Ben and Amy stop eating and look at each other and simultaneously turn to Jimmy.

"He said that?" Amy says. "That's funny, he told me he doesn't have any kids. He told you he has a son your age, huh?"

Jimmy nods, shrugs, and nods again—his usual answer for most questions these days.

"Wonder why he told me he doesn't have kids?"

"He's in boarding school…somewhere out east," Jimmy says. "Why are all the boarding schools out east? Don't we have boarding schools here in Minnesota?"

"Which school is he in, did he mention?" Amy asks.

Jimmy shrugs, he shakes his head this time.

"What he meant was he doesn't have kids living with him," Ben says. "I'm quite sure that's what he meant."

Jimmy reaches for the bowl of mashed potatoes and splats a second heavy scoop on his plate. Ben wonders how someone his size can pack away that much starch and stay skinny as a breadstick. A life of non-stop activity, that's how. Football and now hockey. He is living in Minnesota—the State of Hockey—after all. Years of pond hockey on one of the Bluff's two lakes all winter long. Minnesota, The Land of Ten Thousand Lakes. Lots to pick from, that's for sure. Now he's in his third year of high school hockey, wiry as a steel spring and solid as a ball bearing.

"He's a writer," Amy says to Jimmy. "Did he tell you?"

"Mystery stories," Jimmy replies.

"Mystery *books*," Amy says.

"Oh," Jimmy says, indifferently.

2

After dinner, Ben sits out back and works on a beer. The day is hot, the evening still holds the heat long after the sun has passed. Holds it like a cast iron skillet after the flame is gone. It feels good to be sitting, doing nothing, thinking a little, enjoying the warmth.

Someone walks up the driveway. He enters the backyard and comes straight over and holds out a hand. "Victor Cartuso," he says, amicably.

"Ben Malone." He offers Victor a lawn chair and pulls a beer from the cooler.

"Now that's neighborly...thanks. Hope you don't mind me stopping by like this, unannounced."

"No such thing as unannounced in the Bluff. That's what we call it...the Bluff," Ben explains. "Or me, I call it the burg now and then."

"That's nice, about the neighborly thing, I mean. You'd

never do it in New York, invade someone's space. But somehow I figured here in—"

"You figured right. Gates are always open in the Bluff."

Victor pops the tab off the beer and takes a slow easy hit.

"Wife tells me you're a writer," Ben says.

Victor laughs. He angles his head back and looks up. You can tell he's heard some version of that a million times before. "So I am," he replies with a light groan. "I hear you got the Shell station over on Franklin Street."

"Do indeed. I can get you a real good tune-up for one of those books of yours."

Victor laughs hard and deep. "Now *there's* a bargain I can't pass up. I'll come out ahead on *that* deal for sure."

Ben sets his empty beer can on the lawn. His habit is to line them up next to him, and then when the line gets too long, he grabs a couple and drops them in the recycle container next to the garage. He pulls a new beer from the ice chest and pops the top.

"Mystery novels, huh?" Ben says. "Mystery novels. Where do you guys get your ideas? I always wonder about that when a I read a book. Where do writers get their ideas…especially mystery novels." Ben takes a long pull of beer. "What about you, where do you get your ideas?"

"From everyday life mostly," Victor insouciantly replies. "Then you build a story around it. But that part's pretty easy."

"And then you've got to sell this book…this story you have. Right?" Ben says.

Victor slinks down in the chair a notch. "Uh-huh. You

need an agent, and they find you an editor and a publisher, and everyone hopes the book does well. And maybe you even get lucky and they make it into a movie."

Ben settles on that thought for a second, as if he's listening to a click, click, click of a bad fan belt, and says, "Mysteries sell pretty good, I bet."

"I started out writing horror…you know Stephen King stuff."

"Stephen King! Cripes, Amy's probably read every one of his."

"My first two books were horror." He waves his hand loosely in front of him as though it was something in the distant past, long, long ago. "They did all right. Then I switched and wrote a couple of mysteries and one hit big. They made a movie of it. *Dark Adventure* it was called."

Ben leans forward in his chair. "You're kidding. *You* made that?"

Victor laughs. "Well no, not the *movie*. The movie folks made the movie. I just wrote the book."

"We saw it right here at the multiplex. Believe it or not we do have movies in the Bluff—talkies, no less," Ben says. "Bet you got a pile of money from that."

Victor smiles an indulgent smile but doesn't answer. He looks at the beer can. "Summit…don't think I've heard of it."

"Got a Surly in there, too, if you want," Ben says, pointing to the ice chest. "Summit and Surly, my two favorite Minnesota beers."

"I'm thinking about getting back into horror, just haven't

come up with anything yet."

"Jimmy tells us you got a son about his age."

Victor fiddles with the beer can as though studying it. "Oh…uh-huh…yeah, Matthew. He's in boarding school."

"That's what Jimmy said, but he didn't know where."

"Matthew? Uhm…oh, in uhm, in Exeter…Exeter is where he is. He stays there most of the year. Wasn't so fond of it his first year but loves it now. He might be back for a while this summer. We'll see."

"We could all go fishing together over at the lake," Ben says. "Maybe land a couple of walleye and then Amy can fry them up and we'll have ourselves a real feast.

Victor continues to study the beer. "This is a good beer all right," he says, almost proudly.

"Probably my favorite," Ben says.

"I saw the lakes when I drove in."

"The Bluff has two of 'em…lakes, that is. Cedar Lake and Bluff Lake. If Minnesota has anything, it's lots of lakes. Minnesota and Wisconsin have this old, old contest you might say—who has the most lakes? Wisconsin claims we count mud puddles," Ben says, laughing brightly.

"Yeah, wouldn't mind doing some fishing." Victor sets his empty beer can next to him.

Ben runs his hand inside the cooler and comes up with a Surly. "Here, now try this one…see what you think." He hands it to Victor, then he pulls one out for himself. "You get a big walleye on the line and you know you got a battle. Oh, let me tell you, those babies can get this big." He holds his hands apart wide as his shoulders.

Victor pops open the Surly, takes a sip, and studies the label.

Ben watches him, maybe writers do that—study everything that's written, even beer can labels.

"Another thing to do in the summer is get out that old pontoon and take it over to the river, the Mississippi. I've got one in the garage, a pontoon," Ben says. "Everybody in Minnesota has one, it seems. Now that's a hell of a good time! You can get six people in ours easy. We'll all go over some Saturday or Sunday. You, me, Amy, Jimmy…"

Victor smiles a nod.

"Or we can go to a feed, depending what kind they're having that day."

"A feed?" Victor says, befuddled.

Ben grins. "That's what they call it. A Minnesotan thing where everyone sits around long tables and you eat as much as you want…you know, an all-you-can-eat thing. They call it a feed. There are lots of different kinds of 'em. Smelt feeds, meatball feeds, pancake feeds, and a bunch of others. Me, I'm partial to the smelt feeds…smelt and beans, wow! The pancake feeds are deadly, too. Oh boy, I can eat a *big* stack of those."

Jimmy comes out with a plate of cheese and crackers. "Mom said to bring these to you guys. It's Wisconsin cheese. She told me to tell you that." He sets the plate on the top of the cooler.

"We don't compete with Wisconsin when it comes to cheese making," Ben says. "No, they beat us pretty handily.

Anyway, I can tell you this, it won't take you long to settle into the Bluff, that's for sure."

"I'm giving it six months. I signed a lease with an option to buy after that, if I want." Victor stops talking, his lip curls. He says, "I sorta need to get things rolling again. Been dry as an old beer can. It happens to writers sometimes and let me tell you, it's no fun. Not a bit." He pauses again and looks at Ben. "Imagine if one morning you got up and couldn't remember how to do a tune-up."

Ben groans. "Whew! Now *that* would suck, all right."

"But I've got some good ideas rolling around," Victor says, tapping his head. "I think getting away from New York is gonna make a difference." He slices off a piece of cheddar and picks up a cracker.

3

Ben doesn't encounter Victor again for a full week, but he hears him doing something in the backyard. Building something—pounding and sawing and nailing. He wonders what he's up to but doesn't so much as peek over the fence or between the slats to catch a glimpse of it. He resists the temptation, but it's driving him a little nuts.

Ben mentions it to Amy one morning as she's making breakfast.

Amy cracks an egg into a frying pan. She pulls another one from the carton and drops it on the floor. "Uffdah!" she blurts.

"I got it," Ben says, grabbing a paper towel.

"But I still wonder what he's up to," Ben says, as they sit at the table.

Amy layers a piece of toast with butter, Wisconsin butter. "For Pete's sake, Ben, he just moved in. There're probably a million and one things to do. Don't forget, the Kaminskis, old as they were, did a pretty lousy job of keeping up the property and making repairs."

Ben nods.

"Be happy someone's taking care of the place now even if he's only renting." Amy donates a dollop of strawberry preserves to the toast and takes a small bite. "You two got along real nice the other night."

"Think so. He'll be back, you wait and see. He liked the Summit and the Surly."

"So, where's he from?" Amy says.

"He never really said, exactly. He's been living in New York, or was living in New York. Oh, and his kid, apparently he does have a son about Jimmy's age just like Jimmy said, he's at Exeter."

"Exeter…oh my, that's one of those real snappy schools, isn't it?"

"Putting it mildly," Ben says. "You know, I'm thinking maybe I should stop by and see if he needs help with his project. We've got a basement full of tools, everything you could imagine."

Amy squints. "Ben now, let's not get too Minnesotan on him, okay?" she says, hitting the O of Minnesota long and hard like a true native. "If the other night says anything, I'm sure he'll ask if he needs help. He doesn't seem shy."

Ben heads to work. Warren is talking about some repairs with a customer, discussing a radiator job for an eight-year-old Buick. This is the time of year you make sure the radiator is up to snuff, not in the middle of winter with a blizzard beating down. They're negotiating a price. You negotiate prices in the Bluff. It took Ben a while to get used to that but now it seems to make sense.

When they're finished, Warren says, "That fella from Ohio, the one that moved in next to you, he was in here soon."

"Ohio? What do you mean Ohio? He's from New York,"

"New York, Ohio, maybe…if there is one," Warren says.

Ben looks askance at Warren. "What makes you think that?"

"License plates."

"His car has Ohio plates?"

"Yeup."

"Really!"

"Yeup," Warren says. "You didn't notice?"

"To tell the truth, no. I'm not sure I even know what kinda car he drives. He keeps it in the garage."

Warren wipes his hands on a shop rag. He snags a pack of Marlboros from the shelf behind the counter and taps it three times on his palm and opens it and slips a cigarette part way out and offers it to Ben, knowing full well he won't bite. Courtesy prevails, nonetheless. It's been a struggle for Ben to get to this point, but he made it and all the chicken in General Tso's army can't tempt him to light up now.

Warren sets a match in front of the cigarette and pulls in a drag and blows smoke through his nose.

"So, what did he want?" Ben asks.

"Nothing. Just gassed up, that's all. Said he hadn't seen a full-service station since Nixon swore he wasn't a crook. Said he felt like a king having someone fill his tank for him. Pretty nice Joe, far as I can tell."

Warren cups the cigarette in his palm holding it with his thumb and index finger and pulls in a quick puff, almost snorting. Smoke dribbles from his mouth. He knows the rules: no smoking while pumping gas, no smoking while working in the bays. Too much that can cause everything to go up in a blaze. So he takes advantage of his chances to catch a butt a couple times a day inside the station. Says he likes it better this way. Claims it cuts down on his number of smokes from upwards of a pack a day to less than two packs a week. Pretty soon he'll be doing as good as Ben.

"He's driving out of town for the day," Warren says. "Heading over to Mankato. Seems to know his way around Minnie pretty well."

☐

Back at home that evening, Ben's curiosity wins out. Figuring Victor is gone, he goes to the fence that runs along the garage next to Victor's place. He gawks through a small knothole in one of the slats. The yard looks about as he remembers it when the Kaminskis lived there, all but for something dangling from a beam on the back porch, that is.

Looking through the knothole, he shifts from left eye to right and then back to left again, but he can't tell what it is. He grasps the fence and hoist himself up until his eyes are just above the top.

He's shocked at what he sees. A rope, near as thick as Ben's wrist, is tied in a hangman's noose. It swings limply in the breeze. He lowers himself down. "Wow," he utters silently. He will not divulge this to Amy.

After dinner Ben takes the *Minneapolis Star Tribune* and the cooler and heads out back to bend an elbow. He reads a little from the front page, a little from the Sports section, then sets the paper down. What in Sam Hill is Victor up to, he wonders. Why in the world would he hang a noose from his back porch, and what the hell is all the banging and sawing and nailing of the past several days? Guy doesn't look like the carpenter type; he certainly doesn't have the hands. That's always a dead giveaway. Look at the hands. Guy has the hands of a banker, or a writer, anything but a carpenter.

Ben knows your mind can go real crazy on you when you let it loose. Sitting, taking sips of a Surly now and then. Even so, Ben does some calculating: Victor's back porch is a good three maybe four feet off the ground. If you cut a square in it…and attach a set of hinges at one end…and put in a spring lock at the other—bingo, you've got the perfect backyard gallows. Jesus H! Did he? Could he? Is that what it is? No way.

Ben is tempted to go to the fence and take another look when he hears someone coming up the driveway. Victor Cartuso, of course. He comes around the corner carrying a sixer of Summit.

"Brought you something, Ben," he says. "Ice cold and straight from the Frigidaire."

Frigidaire. Now that's a word Ben hasn't heard in a hell

of a long time, even in a backwater place like Cedar Bluff. He grants Victor a generous smile, opens the cooler, pulls the cans from their plastic holders, and buries them in the ice. He hands one to Victor who is wearing chinos, a short-sleeved shirt—quality, expensive looking—deck shoes, no socks, and a New York Yankees baseball cap. Victor slouches in a chair.

Ben wants to ask him about the noose, but he holds off. Victor is a writer and Ben knows nothing about the writer's mind. Besides, didn't he say he gets his ideas, his writing ideas, from everyday life? And didn't he say he's planning to get back into horror, as he put it? Well…maybe this is it. It would fit, wouldn't it, Ben surmises. Even so, Ben feels quite sure you don't have to hang yourself to write about it. Stupid thing to consider, obviously.

"Took a little trip today," Victor says.

"To Mankato."

Victor tilts toward Ben. "Yep…how'd you know?"

"Warren, at the station."

"Of course," Victor says, slipping slowly back into the chair. He starts talking about the full-service deal at the station and repeats that he hasn't seen that since Nixon swore he's not a crook, just like he told Warren. "Went to pay a visit to an old bookstore in Mankato. Ever been over that way?"

"Mankato? Oh, sure. The Cedar Bluff Tigers play the Mankato Scarlets in hockey every year. Jimmy is a left winger on the Tigers. Kid's got a real sick shot, I might add. That's what the kids call it…a sick shot," he says with a grin.

"Well, this store, the one in Mankato, had a book I've been

after for years, An out-of-print book. Couldn't even find it on Amazon. Huh! When you can't do that you know you're pretty much SOL. So, the thing to do is start scoping out the old stores. I knew there was a good one in Mankato. It's called Mason's Books."

For want of something to say, Ben asks if Victor's had a chance to do any writing yet.

Victor studies his Summit can, this time rather half-heartedly, then looks up to about the height of the roof of the house and calmly says, "Not yet. Still clearing out the old cobwebs." He taps his head gently along his temple. "It's coming though…it's coming," he adds in a very unconvincing way. He looks over at Ben, takes a sip of beer and says, "Let me ask you something, I need to find a place to work out, you know, to get some exercise. I want to be in shape before I…well, let's just say I have a big project that'll take all my strength and I need to be in shape."

"Me, I'm over at the gym on Fourteenth Street a couple times a week. The gym-*nauseum*, I tell Amy. A couple miles on the *dread*-mill, I tell her. When you go through as many crappy lunches as I do in a week, the burgers and the fries I mean, heart-attack-in-a-sack is what I call it, when you do that often enough, you need to find a way to keep the old ticker purring. Lately, I've been trying to get home for lunch to beat the trans-fat game."

"While we're at it, I've got another favor," Victor says.

"Shoot."

"I'm doing some work on the house. Some repairs…you

know, uhm, fixing things up a bit, that kind of stuff. Would you happen to have a power saw; one of those circular gizmos? I'm getting blisters using that old hand saw. And you don't get a very good cut with it, not real straight." He holds his palm out and shows the blister.

Sure enough just as Ben suspected, it's the hand of a banker or a writer, maybe an accountant, certainly not a carpenter.

"Do I have a saw? Cripes I practically have an entire Menards down there," referring to the basement. "If I don't have it, they don't make it. You betcha…you can borrow anything you want."

Victor trolls for a beer and snags a Surly. "Let me tell you, it's certainly nice out here in the evenings. You guys have a hell of a good summer."

Ben chortles. "Well, we don't have much of a spring, and fall is pretty but short. It's sorta like what we Chicagoans used to say back when I lived there. We'd say, oh sure, we have seasons. Four of 'em—winter, winter, winter, and road construction."

Victor laughs.

"No road construction here, but just wait till January and February roll around, see what you think about the weather then."

"Witches tit in a brass bra?"

"Worse. Thor's nuts in tin cup."

Victor Cartuso likes the analogy; he claims Ben could be a writer.

In return, Ben tells him he actually went all the way through four years of college at DePaul University in Chicago and came out with a degree in history. Says he doesn't read many novels, Amy does.

"I have a big bookshelf full of biographies and a bunch on World War II, the stuff I like the most," Ben says. "But when we moved to the Bluff there wasn't much to do with a history degree. Thought of getting into the insurance business or some dreary thing like that. Then Amy heard that the gas station on Franklin Street was up for grabs. Hell, I could take a car apart and put it back together blindfolded when I was twelve years old. That's how it happened. That's how I ended up with the Shell."

"Well the good thing about being a writer is you can work anywhere. These days all you need is a computer and the internet."

Ben sets an empty can on the ground and pulls an ice-cold Summit from the cooler. Victor must have turned that old Frigidaire the Kaminskis left down to zero. Ben holds the can to his side and snaps the top; it squirts and fizzes.

"Oh incidentally, I want to mention I'm going out of town for a few days," Victor says. "Uhm…to New York to see my agent. Claims she can peddle one of my old books as a new release, yada, yada, yada." Victor shakes his head. "Those people are always scheming. Anyway, I was wondering if you might pick up my mail and put it inside. I'll leave a key for you."

"Done," Ben says with a toast of his Summit.

4

The next day a Menards truck pulls up in front of Victor's house. Ben watches as two guys climb out and take a stack of plywood and load of two-by-fours and carry them to the garage where Victor is waiting. He signs a sheet of paper and promptly lowers the door.

Ben loaned Victor the circular saw—two, actually. He has three beauties to pick from: one with a coarse blade for cutting thick wood, one with a medium blade for cutting smaller pieces, one with a fine blade for finish cutting. Rather than change blades, Ben has the whole set. Victor selected the coarse one and the medium one.

Ben puts on his green Minnesota Wild cap and drives to work. Victor has yet to leave the house key with Ben, and he never said for sure when he was going. "In a couple of days," is what Ben recalls.

Later that morning, Amy goes down Highway 22 to the Barnes & Noble over in Owatonna, about thirty miles east. She walks down the Fiction and Literature aisle until she reaches the section with the authors whose name begins with C. Sure enough, there they are, lots of books by Victor Cartuso. It's for real, all right. She pulls out her cell phone and takes a picture of the whole line of them that she'll show Ben when she gets back. Better yet, she takes one of each of the books and totes the tall stack to the checkout.

"Oh, ye-uh…these are Victor Cartusos. I love 'em," the girl at the register says, running the books one by one through the scanner. "We can barely keep 'em on the shelf. This one here, this one's my favorite. Oh…it was good, all right."

Amy smiles, hands the girl her Mastercard. She says nothing about Victor moving in next to them over in Cedar Bluff. She takes the bag of books and goes to the Starbucks that's part of the bookstore. It's a requirement—a law, it seems—Barnes & Noble and Starbucks. Sort of like La Quinta and Denny's. She gets a tall latte and begins to read one of the books.

About one o'clock, shortly after Amy gets back from Owatanna, Ben returns home for a bun—Minnesotan for a sandwich. In this case tuna, with a side of fruit.

"Went to the bookstore over there in Owatonna," Amy says. "Figured if we're ever invited over to his place, I ought to know a little about his work, him being a writer and all." She sits down and picks up half a sandwich and a dill wedge.

"And?" Ben asks, still not thoroughly convinced Victor is truly a writer.

"And what?"

"Whad'ya find?"

"Lots." Amy gets iced tea from the refrigerator. She sits down and pulls her phone from her purse and shows Ben the picture she took in the bookstore.

Ben takes the phone. "Geez Louise," he utters. "Those are his?"

"Lots of 'em lined up one after another. Lots." She holds her hands a foot and a half apart or so.

"No shit."

"Fourteen different books. Is that for real or what? Fourteen. And we're talking real good stuff. I read a bunch in one of them while I was having a latte. Mostly mysteries of one kind or another. There's this whole series about this cop guy that's always tracking down some deranged killer. The titles are *Dark* this and *Dark* that. And right there on the back of each is a picture of Victor. Our Victor!" she says. "A pretty darn good picture, I must say—younger but you can tell right away it's him."

"No shit," Ben says again, rather stunned by the news. "I was beginning to think he's been bamboozling me, telling me he's a writer when he's not. When you're talking to him, he never quite seems to be in the moment…not fully anyway. Like he's off on a thought somewhere." Ben waves his hand as if he's referring to someplace in outer space.

"Well, we now have nearly the total collection of Victor Cartuso novels because I bought all fourteen. It was kind of spendy," Amy says. "But if nothing else, that should keep me going near till Christmas…could be beyond."

Before heading back to work, Ben stops in the living room

and looks at the stack of Cartuso books. Turning one over, he sees the picture of Victor. Yep…that's him, all right, Ben assures himself. You can't mistake that mug, those sleepy almost droopy eyes. Looking like he's buried in thought, just like when he's out in the backyard pulling on a beer, talking about nothing at all. That's Victor Cartuso, all right.

New York Times Bestselling Author, it boasts on the cover. Ben stares at it for a while, then begins to page through. Just as Amy said, there's a cop, a guy named Bill Barker, in a small town in Ohio of all places, not in New York or LA like most of the other detective stories you read these days. It's the same cop character, Bill Barker, that was in the *Dark Adventure* movie that Ben and Amy saw at the Bluff's multiplex. He doesn't remember who played the part of Barker. Could have been Robert De Niro or Al Pacino, but it could have been someone else, a big name.

Picking up several other books Ben sees they're part of the mystery series Amy told him about. They all have Bill Barker hot on the tail of some bad-ass killer.

Ben starts reading a bit from one of the books. Nice stuff, I could enjoy this, he tells himself. It reminds him a lot of Raymond Chandler's work, without doubt Ben's favorite detective writer. Bill Barker is out of the Philip Marlowe mold. Anyone who can write like Chandler gets my vote. This Barker guy seems real hard-boiled, fond of his bourbon, just like Marlowe.

Ben grabs one of the books randomly, *Dark Winter*, and shoves it in his back pocket. "Heading out," he says to Amy as he leaves.

When he gets to the station, Warren is ringing up a bill for a customer. He probably just came off a smoke break; Ben detects the lingering bouquet of nicotine in the air. They talk for a couple of minutes about what's going on in the bay. One job, minor, oil change, tune up, rotate the tires, put a new one on the left front.

Ben goes out to gas up a customer. The locals know to stay put and wait for someone from the station to come out. All the lanes say Full Service even though the gas is priced just like at the self-service joints. And full-service means a quick wash and squeegee across the front and back windows in the summer, and a scrape of ice in the winter. You can be sure it makes a difference when the temperature hits minus thirteen.

In the station Ben hands Warren the Cartuso book.

"Now this is the kind of thing I could enjoy," Warren says, paging through it. "A cop chasing down some wacko. Of course you *know*, don't you, the cop's gonna win in the end. When don't they? The guys in the white hat *always* win, right? That's the rule, isn't it?"

Ben gives that a bit of thought and says, "Now there's a good twist for you, let the evil dude win." He thinks again and says, "Nah…nah, that won't work."

For a moment, he wonders if Cartuso ever considered flipping a story like that. He did say his ideas come from everyday life and, yes unfortunately, really unfortunately, the bad guys do come out ahead now and then. In fact, there are some great works of fiction where that did indeed happen. Take *Body Heat*, for example, Matty Walker pulls off the perfect murder.

Or some of Stephen King's horror—*Thinner* and *Pet Sematary*—no smiley faces waiting at the end of those.

Warren wipes his hands on a rag and returns to the bay. Ben sits in the tattered red vinyl rescue chair behind the counter and reads the first page of the book. Bill Barker wakes up with a bad headache and a bad case of amnesia and he's not sure why. Was it a long night with the bottle, or a bad cuff he took on the head? He looks at himself in the mirror, not happy with what he sees.

Twice Ben does the full-service thing then returns to the book. Before he knows it, he's forty-five pages in. For someone who rarely reads novels, this one is tough to put down. Barker's having a tough time. His frequent rendezvous with Rock and Rye is a pretty good promo for temperance.

☐

After dinner Ben retreats to the backyard. He's barreling fast through *Dark Winter*.

Victor doesn't make an appearance. By nine o'clock Ben is almost done with the book. Barker and Slime, that's what Barker calls the killer, are head-to-head in an old warehouse. Forty pages of this until there they are, alone in a large empty room with cracked and broken windows along one wall, and little else. Slime has his 9 mm Ruger aimed straight at Barker. He pulls the trigger. A bullet sails through Barker's chest, through the bottom lobe of his right lung but spares all the important real estate. Barker gasps, leans over, and sucks wind.

Slime fires again. His gun jams; he pounds the barrel onto his palm. Barker unloads a clip from his Glock 21 into Slime.

Barker lives to fight another day.

Ben smiles and pulls a Surly from the cooler.

5

Ben has seen not hide nor hair of Victor for three days, but he hears one hell of a lot of pounding and banging coming from next door. Victor is certainly putting the skill saws to good use working on something inside the house, this time down in the basement, by all accounts.

It's Wednesday at nine in the morning. Everything at the Shell is rolling along fine. Two cars in for repairs, one in each bay. Ben does a front-end alignment while Warren is buried under the dashboard of a Jeep trying to figure why the panel lights have gone south. It might seem like the easier of the two jobs, but Ben hates poking around with fuses, testing them, tracking down tangled wires. Warren has a knack for it.

"Car's coming in later for suspensions," Warren tells Ben. "Starting to get a lot of 'em now what with old 32 over there tore up as she is."

The bell rings in the bay; someone in for gas. Ben looks out at the car. "Well don't you know it, Victor Cartuso," he tells Warren.

Warren cranes to catch a glimpse as though Cartuso is a celebrity. And in a sense he is, from what Warren knows so far.

Ben wipes his hands and goes to the pump.

"Hey there pal. Gas 'er up, old buddy," Victor says.

Ben starts the pump.

"I'm heading up to the airport, up in Minneapolis," Victor says, calling out the window. "Be gone a few days. Think you'll have the time to take care of the mail?"

"Good grief, of course," Ben says. "This is…"

"Let me guess, Cedar Bluff. Did I get it right?"

Ben laughs. Maybe he's worn that one out a bit.

"The key to the front door," Victor says, holding it out the window. "Leave the mail and the newspaper on the dining room table."

"Got it." Ben gives the gas cap a twist until it clicks three times. He takes the key and a credit card from Victor and goes in and rings up the gas. "You have a safe trip now," he tells Victor, handing him his card.

Victor gives a thumbs up.

"Oh, and good luck with that agent thing," Ben says. Victor delivers another thumbs up.

Ben watches as he drives off; he notices the license plate. Ohio, just as Warren had said. When Victor's halfway down the street, Ben remembers he meant to tell him he read one of his books.

Back in the bay, the day's heat is coming on fast.

"Get ready, gonna be a hot one," Ben tells Warren as he

turns on the large fan that pulls air through the bay.

Warren climbs out from under the dashboard—panel lights fixed. He pulls the Jeep out, parks it in the lot, goes in for a smoke, pours a cup of three-hour-old coffee from the Krups, and has a Ho-Ho.

Ben wipes sweat off his forehead. "Whew, now that's what I call heat," he says, looking out at the sky and feeding a dollar into the soda machine. He mops his forehead again. "So…how's the weekend sizing up?" he asks Warren.

"Oooh…pretty fair, I guess. Sunday, we'll be at my folks for dinner. Jennifer's bringing a hot dish…Sis, some barbeque is my guess."

Ben knows enough Minnesotan to translate this into a casserole and Sloppy Joes.

"You folks?"

"Not sure," Ben says. "A little trolling out on Cedar or Bluff would be nice. Keeping it easy and light, that's the plan." He downs half the Coke.

☐

Ben is home at five-fifteen. His evening routine is simple. Before doing anything, he's in the shower to scour the day's grease from his hands and nails and hair.

He goes to Victor's to collect the mail. There isn't much, a couple of bills, more than a couple of flyers. "Too bad for mailmen these days," Ben mumbles, "deliver more crap than mail."

Inside, he places the mail on the dining room table exactly as Victor requested. Turning to leave, curiosity grabs him. Shouldn't do this, I know, he tells himself. But, hey, can't hurt to peek out the back door, maybe see what the guy's been up to the past few days. What can it matter when you consider I could just as easily find out by looking over the fence?

The kitchen is not much different from when the Kaminskis lived there. If Victor is a great writer, he is clearly no culinary wizard.

Ben looks out the window onto the back porch. The noose is gone; he feels instantly better. And the fact that Victor hasn't built a trap door below where the noose had been makes Ben feel better yet. "Okay, enough damn snooping." Turning to leave he sees a receipt for a pair of air tickets on the kitchen table. "Huh…must be for the trip." In large letters he sees the word DEPART MSP-Minneapolis/Saint Paul, ARRIVE CMH-Columbus. A reservation for National Car Rental, too.

Yikes, Victor is going to Columbus, Ben surmises. Surely, he's not going to drive from Columbus, Ohio to New York City. Is he? Next to the airline info is a reservation at the Marriott in Zanesville, Ohio. So…he *is* going to Ohio. What happened to New York? Fuck it, Ben, none of your goddamn business, dude.

Passing through the dining room, he sees a small framed newspaper clipping on the bureau. Bending over, hands on his knees, he reads it. It's from the Zanesville newspaper—the Obit section—it describes the death of a Matthew Scott

Cartuso, hanged in the garage at the age of twelve. It says nothing other than that the matter is still under investigation. Ben looks for a date but doesn't see one. From the condition of the clipping's dull and faded appearance he guestimates it to be two to three years old.

He's creeped out by the bone-chilling information and ticked at himself for snooping. Looking around, he sees that Victor has turned the dining room into a writing nook—laptop, printer, lots of paper, crap like that.

He leaves and locks the door.

Each day Ben does exactly as promised—picks up the mail and the newspaper, sets them on the dining room table, leaves and locks up.

6

Victor returns from his trip four days later and pulls into his garage around six-thirty in the evening. After dinner, Ben picks up the sports section and ambles out to the backyard and pops a beer. Like clockwork, the sound of footsteps is heard coming up the driveway. Victor, for sure.

Ben folds the paper and sets it on the ground. Victor comes over and gives a, "Hey, pal." He pushes a chummy smile, but it's not all that convincing.

"Saved you a chair and ordered you a cold one," Ben tells Victor, holding out a beer. Victor's smile improves. He sits down but doesn't say much for a while. Ben has a pretty good idea Victor's waiting for him to get things rolling. "How'd the trip go?"

Victor lets out a groan that says a lot. "Ah, it was fine…I suppose. You know what traveling is like these days…damn exhausting. Waiting in lines at the airport, going through all that TSA crap, take off the belt, take off the shoes. Next thing you know they'll make us strip down to nothing and put on one of those paper hospital gowns, the ones that tie in back. Won't *that* be a moment to endure! And then, of course, there's always some butthead in line behind you who's pissed because he's about to miss his plane…like it's my fault, *my* fault, right?"

Ben smirks. Victor nailed that perfectly, he did.

"And, see, I have this old bag that I've used for years. You know, one of those thick cloth sorts of things with two belts that fasten on the outside, kind of like something you'd use on steerage in the old days crossing the Atlantic or something. Well, of course, they treat it like it's full of kryptonite, or whatever."

Ben smiles, it draws a perfect picture in his mind.

"There was once a time when air travel was something to enjoy. Remember?" Victor continues. "Now they treat you like you're boarding a Greyhound for Gary, Indiana, or somewhere. Oh well, maybe it's better this way. It is cheaper than it was twenty or thirty years ago. I guess that makes it worth it…I suppose."

Ben tells Victor he read one of his books. Victor perks up. He says it was *Dark Winter* and he liked what Victor did with Bill Barker, how he made him believable, very Chandleresque.

Victor lifts an eyebrow and slumps down in his chair and studies his beer can once again. "Raymond Chandler, now that's a guy who knew how to string words together, all right. A real wordsmith. I love his work." A sip of beer and he adds, "I have to confess though, *Dark Winter* isn't one of my favorite books. You get pushed into doing crap sometimes, especially when you've had a couple of good books recently. The agents, the editors, the publishers, they can turn you into a first-class whore if you're not careful. They're on your ass to get the next book out even if you're not happy with it. It's all part of the shtick, I suppose."

"Well I sure liked it," Ben tells him. "And now I'm ready for another."

"You want to know which one is the best of the bunch?" Victor says, "besides *Dark Adventure*, of course. *Dark Temptation*…give that a try."

Ben remembers seeing it among the stack Amy brought home.

Almost immediately, Victor changes the subject. The words come out as though they are the real reason for his visit.

"Ben, there's something I need to say, something I need to get off my chest. I feel real shitty because I misled you about my son…Matthew." Victor breathes deeply and stops talking for a moment. Ben waits. Victor looks more pensive than ever. "Well, he's not at Exeter, Matthew I mean…you see…Matthew, Matthew's dead."

It's exactly what Ben already knew, having seen the clipping in his house, but he tries to act surprised.

"It's been a couple of years now, three to be exact. It's very hard to talk about it so, I dunno, sometimes I just make up a story about him still being at Exeter. He was going to school there." Victor looks at Ben as if he's seeking forgiveness for his lie.

Ben doesn't think of it as a lie, not exactly. Well, yes, it is of course, but some things in life are off limits to the general public. Ben knows that. It's just that now Ben will have to break the news to Amy and Jimmy about Victor's son.

Victor sighs. In a despairing voice, he says, "They say he hanged himself."

Weird choice of words, Ben thinks. How can you not know? Then it hits him, maybe it wasn't suicide. Is that what he's getting at? He feels a chill run through him and thinks about the comment in the Obit, the one saying that Matthew's death was still under investigation. Did someone hang the poor kid and try to make it look like suicide?

"This happened in Zanesville…in Ohio. Marla, my wife, she, uh…she passed away a while back, see, we were originally from Zanesville. We had a house there. Not the kind of town most people want to live in…old rust belt joint, but sometimes it's hard to let go of your past. For me it is."

"I still think about Chicago now and again."

Victor nods. "Of course, after the bucks started rolling in from the Bill Barker books and the movie they made, we got ourselves a place in New York on the upper East Side. Yeah. But we're a real restless bunch, aren't we? We Americans, I mean. The problem is that when you leave something behind and then, later, try to come back to it, you find that it *ain't* the same as it was before. Like Thomas Wolfe told us in his book, *You Can't Go Home Again*."

Ben has a half dozen questions he'd like to ask Victor, but

he doesn't. He can tell Victor is the kind of guy that lets information out a little at a time. Yet, in a crazy way, Victor seems lifted by the chance to clear the record about his son—the way you feel when you pay a visit to a shrink or go to confession. I guess your shrink is wherever you find him. In this case, in the backyard slumped in a lawn chair next to a cooler of beer. Why the fuck not!

"So I went back to Zanesville to take care of some business and put the place up for sale. I'm ready to leave it, ready to try and put the whole sad episode behind me. To salvage my life if I can."

Victor pulls out a pack of cigarettes, a new unopened pack. He unzips the red cellophane strip around the top and stops and says, "Oh, sorry, do you mind?"

Ben tells him it's okay, and tells him about Warren at the Shell, and says he himself managed to give up the nicotine a while ago.

"I don't smoke, not very often. Hardly ever, in fact. Only when I'm upset...upset like now."

Victor takes a cigarette and lights it with a plastic BIC lighter and slips the pack in his shirt pocket. He grabs onto a long deep breath and turns his head away and blows smoke off to the side. He does this a second time almost immediately, filling his lungs and quickly emptying them, then sits with the cigarette dangling from his fingers until he eventually buries the tip of it in the grass. He gets up and tosses the butt in the trash can and pulls the practically full pack from his shirt and donates it to the can as well.

"Done!" he says firmly, returning and sitting down. "Won't have another one of those for a month, maybe never."

Like a good shrink, Ben glances casually in Victor's direction off and on. If he wants to talk about Zanesville and the house and his son—fine. Victor is the decider. If he's done with it—fine.

It turns out Victor's done with it for now. He gradually starts talking about writing. True, Ben doesn't know shinola about writing, but of course he knows even less about shrinking. Though he is a good listener, so says Amy.

"When I was flying back, I came up with an idea for a novel, at least I think so. Something always happens to me when I'm up there at thirty-nine thousand feet. My mind empties out and my thinking becomes more clear. Maybe the air is different, I don't know. It comes from outside the plane, doesn't it? Or is it the same air that was in the plane when you took off?"

"Good question."

"Well, whichever it is, I can tell you I think very differently when I'm wedged into that crappy little seat looking out the window at the ground far below. A thought, an idea, pops into my head and I focus on it for a *long* time." He reaches over and selects a beer from the cooler and holds it out and lift the pop-top...*ffsssst.*

"A new book, huh? A Bill Barker?"

"Nope. No more Bill Barkers, not for a while at least."

"That horror thing?" Ben asks.

Victor doesn't answer immediately. Then as if he can't

hold out anymore, he smiles a bit and says. "Think so." Suddenly, Victor's in pretty good spirits. Maybe the smoke helped, or maybe just talking with Ben about writing helped.

As Ben sees it, there are at least two sides to this guy. The Victor that's quiet, serious, and off somewhere deep in thought. And then there is the writer Victor—the engaged and animated chap. It's a funny mix.

"I'll be at it on the laptop good and early tomorrow," Victor says. "That's when I work best."

"So, do you have this thing outlined or whatever…the story?"

"Oh, Christ no, I never write that way. I have some vague ideas about what's gonna happen, where it will happen, crap like that. Some of the characters. But the rest just rolls out as I go along." He pantomimes as if he's typing. It paints a good picture.

Ben shakes his head. "Crazy."

7

Saturday morning. Ben tells Amy and Jimmy about Matthew being dead. It's a total shock, especially to Jimmy. He can't fathom why Victor didn't tell them that in the beginning.

Ben tries to provide a rationalization, but Jimmy isn't buying it, so Ben tells him it's the way people sometimes deal with trouble in their life, and he claims that everyone twists the truth now and then, everyone…yes, even Jimmy. He gives an example of how when they ask him if he's done his homework, he says he has when he hasn't.

"That's homework," Jimmy argues. "Mr. Cartuso is talking about someone who's dead, for the love of Mike." A term he picked up from his father but would never be caught using in front of his friends.

Later on, to get Jimmy out of his funk, Ben takes him and one of his friends fishing on Cedar Lake. Being the bigger of the two lakes, you have a better chance of landing something that'll give a good fight, maybe a walleye or a large mouth bass or a northern pike even, if the gods are shining down. If not, you're still likely to come home with a couple of crappies, some bluegill and pumpkinseed, some perch.

But Cedar Lake is not gigantic, not like the bigger holes that are the choice of the water skiers and speed boaters. And that's exactly what Ben likes about their lakes. Both of them, Cedar Lake and Bluff Lake, are perfect for lazy fishing—the only kind Ben ascribes to.

Ben considered offering Victor a chance to join them, the boat being big enough to easily handle four, but Victor has been mostly off the radar for the past few days. Ben figures he's burning words on his laptop, though at one point he heard the buzz of the skill saw followed by a couple minutes of pounding.

The fishing is going well, nothing much but a steady string of pan fish. They'll keep enough to put on the grill and set the rest free. You have to eat them fresh, that's the whole point.

All three have a line in the water now. Langford, Jimmy's friend, is using a lure, a jig. He's hoping to land a walleye. He casts a half dozen times and slowly reels in giving the lure a series of small jerks. You can tell the kid's done this before.

Suddenly, he feels a hit. You're never sure in these old lakes if you've snagged a stick or twig until you get some movement of the line. Sure enough, whatever Lang has, it ain't the bottom on the lake. He feeds out a short stretch of line.

Ben glances over. "Ou-wee, get a load of that!" he tells Jimmy. "Lang's got something. Keep 'er going, Lang, you're doing great."

He's using a four-pound test and a Fenwick Walleye Series rod. A good choice. It allows lots of play for the fish and lots of challenge for the fisherman. If he has a nice walleye, a keeper let's say, he's got his hands full. It'll be a challenge but a hell of a lot of fun.

Lang is no slouch, he's working the fish like a pro. Letting a little line out but keeping it taut. You give it too much slack and off goes your catch once it slips the hook. Lang raises the rod. It's as bent as a quarter moon. Oh yeah, he's got a damn good something or other on the end.

"Go, Lang, go!" Jimmy says as though he's calling to him from the bench at one of their hockey games, as though Lang's racing down the ice on a breakaway about to fire off one of his sick snapshots.

"You're doing great, Lang," Ben adds. "Don't let it break the line on you...give a little."

The fish circles back and comes over to the other side of the boat. Lang follows perfectly. "Okay, here we go," he says. "I think I can bring her in." He reels gently until the fish is just blow the edge of the boat.

Jimmy takes a net and slips it quickly under the fish and pulls it up.

"Oh boy," Jimmy crows. "She's a beaut!" He knows immediately it's a keeper, but he measures just the same. "Oh wow, well over the fifteen minimum."

"You're gonna bring home some real good dinner tonight," Ben tells Lang, who smiles broad and wide. Jimmy snaps a picture with his phone of Lang holding his haul.

They stay at it for another hour and a half, no more wall-eye, mostly crappie, both black and white and an occasional bluegill and pumpkinseed. They keep enough crappie for a meal and the rest go back in the water.

The day's heat is strong. Ben could use an ice-cold one but he never brings beer on these outings with the kids. Being on the lake can be worse than rush hour traffic in the city. Lots of blockheads getting tanked up; it's not the kind of message Ben wants to leave with Jimmy and Lang.

Occasionally, when Ben's out with Warren, they'll cart a cooler, but even then they go slow and keep their wits.

On shore, Ben cleans the fish for Lang. They bring the fillets home on ice. Jimmy is invited to share Lang's big catch that night. The fish will be perfect for Lang and his parents and Jimmy.

"Mom makes a real good dipped walleye," Lang boasts: batter-fried in Minnesota parlance.

8

Monday afternoon. Jimmy Malone comes home from school at three-thirty. His parents are at work. Good time to shoot hoops. Unlocking the side door to the garage, he is greeted by all the familiar smells: old wood, fragrances emitted from the lawnmower and leaf blower and weed eater. The delicate scents of lake and river water that are forever seared into the cushions and planks of the pontoon. And somewhere in all of that is the basketball and the hand pump. Jimmy always pumps the ball tight as a melon—nothing worse than a quaggy basketball.

He flips the light switch and begins looking for the ball when he is stopped in his tracks. Dangling from a ceiling beam is a rope as thick as Jimmy's wrist with a noose tied at the end. He stares at it for a long time.

But it's not just a rope and a noose. The whole affair is strung above a skinny stool some three feet tall. Jimmy walks slowly toward it, trying to figure out how all this got into their locked garage.

Reaching up, he grabs the rope and gives a sharp snap. It doesn't budge a millimeter. He lets go and crosses his arms.

Stepping back, he thinks he should never have touched it in the first place. "No way Dad would have put this thing here," he tells himself. He tugs again, this time pulling harder. "Whoa…whoever put this up, meant it for real!"

Little by little, curiosity starts to weigh in. Jimmy gives the stool a nudge. It wobbles but seems otherwise stable.

He puts a foot on top, waits, then steps up. The stool wiggles precariously for a second, tilting slightly to the side as if one leg is a fraction shorter than the others. He holds his arms out and does a momentary tightrope act to get his balance as he looks at the concrete floor below him.

Grabbing the noose with both hands, he pulls on it, gently at first then harder and harder until almost all his weight is supported by it. "Cripes, you could string King Kong up on this little gem," he says beneath his breath.

He has an urge to put the noose over his head to imagine what it might feel like to be up on the gallows. He tries to shake the thought from his mind but the temptation is too great. He stuffs his head through the noose, knees bent to give him better balance like when he's ice skating.

He tightens the slip knot gently under his chin—no harm done. For no rational reason other than that he is sixteen years old, he places his hands behind his back and pretends he's about to be hanged, thinking he's been given one last breath of fresh air before he leaves the planet forever.

He stares solemnly ahead as if waiting for the hangman to drop the door beneath his feet. Then, at that very second, his balance shifts.

The stool wobbles and shakes. Sideways, backwards. The noose pulls tighter around his neck. Reaching awkwardly, he grabs the rope while trying desperately to regain his balance.

A moment of panic overtakes him as he pictures himself suspended from the ceiling, grasping the rope. It squeezes tighter on his neck as he tries to free himself from the noose.

At last, he steadies himself on the rickety stool and rips the rope from his head. "*Muh-tha fucker!*" he blurts, jumping off the stool and landing safely on the hard concrete.

Stepping back, he watches the noose sway—almost angrily—in front of him. Nervous and scared, he abandons his plans to shoot hoops. He locks the garage and goes in the house.

By four-thirty, Amy is home. Shortly after, Ben comes in whistling a happy tune. He heads to the backyard to check the tomato plants. Jimmy follows.

"What's up kiddo," Ben says, looking at a near-ripe beefsteak. "Want me to beat you in a game of HORSE, is that it?"

Jimmy laughs awkwardly. "Nah…here, Dad, let me show you something."

"Uh-huh, what?"

"Over here." Jimmy retrieves the garage key from his pocket, opens the door, and flicks the light switch.

Ben, right behind, stares at the noose in the middle of the room. "Geez Louise," he moans softly, watching as the noose dangles imperceptibly in the draught garage air. He walks toward it. Stopping a couple feet away, he turns to Jimmy and says, "What's this all about?" as if Jimmy might know.

Jimmy shrugs. "It was here when I came in to get the basketball."

Ben looks at the noose. "You're kidding."

"Who would put a thing like that in our garage?" Jimmy asks. "And, anyway, how'd they get in? The door was all locked up."

Ben rubs his forehead. He reaches down and presses on the stool. "You didn't mess with this now, did you? I mean get up on it or anything?"

"Come on, Dad."

"Or put your head in it?" He points at the noose.

"Come on, Dad."

"Well, I hope not." Ben reaches and grabs the noose just as Jimmy had done. "That thing's up there, all right." He puts both hands on the stool and presses down hard. "Oh boy, now that fella has a real wobble to it...not good at all." He picks the stool up and turns it over and rubs his thumb across one of the legs. "Looks to be someone cut this one down a smidge...see that? Sure would make the whole thing real shaky if you got up on it. We're talking real dangerous." He looks at Jimmy and says, "Someone gets up on the stool goofing off, puts their head in that thing, and this baby starts shaking and...bam. We won't go there, okay?"

Ben pulls his cell phone from his pocket and snaps a round of pictures of the garage gallows from three or four angles, then opens a step ladder and inspects the top of the rope. It's wrapped a half dozen times around the beam; the end is nailed to the beam itself. There's not a millimeter of slack in it.

"If someone were to find themselves dangling from that rope, it would end pretty quick," Ben says, from up on the ladder. "Whoever did this knew what they were doing. This thing here is no joke."

Ben gets a hammer and screwdriver and pries loose the end of the rope. He inspects the large ten-penny nails used to hold it to the beam and puts the nails in his pocket.

"You gonna tell the police?" Jimmy asks.

Ben doesn't answer. He unravels the rope and removes it from the beam and climbs off the ladder. "Not sure," he says.

"It seems like they'd want to see it. Don't you think?" Jimmy says.

Ben knows it's not that simple. For just a moment he wonders if Victor Cartuso had a hand in this…but why? Victor's friendship with Ben has become down-right pleasant.

"This much is for sure, your mother is not gonna get wind of this…capiche?"

Jimmy nods.

"Capiche?" Ben says again.

"Uh-huh," Jimmy replies.

Ben takes the rope and noose and stuffs it into a plastic lawn bag and sets it on a shelf. He has a pretty damn good idea whoever broke into the garage and put up the noose didn't leave many tracks—all it would take was a pair of gloves.

But, of course, how did they get the key for the garage?

9

Ben skips his evening trip to the backyard for his visit with the ice chest and cold beer. It's summer, and in Minnesota you take every advantage of the good weather, but he knows he will have to say something about the garage affair to Victor, his new neighbor, and he's not ready for that quite yet.

He sits in the living room and watches the Twins on TV. They're losing 4-2. Doesn't matter, he's not paying much attention. Amy comes by. She asks if he's all right. He pokes a smile.

"What, not gonna sit out back?"

"Don't know…might," Ben replies.

"Sure is nice out. Quite the day today. Oh, for warm. If you were in the sun is what I mean, of course."

"Say, now you didn't see anything weird in the garage, did you?"

"See anything weird in the garage? No, not really. But

then I didn't go in the garage."

"Well, maybe I *will* go out back." He grabs the ice chest in the kitchen, heads to the backyard, and sits in his favorite lawn chair.

Like clockwork, Ben hears footsteps coming up the drive-way—Victor Cartuso, of course. Victor comes around the corner. One look at his face and you can tell he's in good spirits. He's carrying a sixer of Summit. "Little company, perhaps?" he inquires.

Ben smiles and offers Victor a chair.

"I'm feeling like a million today," Victor says. "I was on a roll all day at the laptop." He does an imitation of himself typing on imaginary keys, fingers jumping up and down. "One of my best days in a long time. You wait for these days when you're a writer. They make up for the ones when you can't scribble out so much as a nursery rhyme."

To Ben, Victor doesn't look like a man who would do something as sinister as what he and Jimmy saw in the garage. If so, he's quite the chameleon.

Victor prattles on for six or seven minutes about his book, then stops abruptly and says. "Look at me, will you. I come over here and what do I do, yak about myself and the stupid books I write." He rolls his eyes.

"It's okay," Ben responds. "I like hearing about book writing…me being part of the lug nut crowd."

"What's up with you…anything new down at the Shell?"

Ben pulls in a long swig of beer. He desperately wants to talk about the noose but can't quite get himself to. Yet, he knows he will have to, eventually. Finally, he says, "I gotta tell you something that happened today. Something real fucked up strange."

Victor figures it must have to do with the Shell, the gas station. A radiator that exploded maybe.

"Well…it was in the garage. Our garage, not at work." He points to the building behind them.

"Uh-huh, what?"

"Oh, geez…someone, I have no idea who, someone strung a rope and a noose from one of the beams in the garage."

Victor rests his forehead on his hand and stares at the ground—silent, motionless.

Of all the things to tell Victor, Ben thinks, something having to do with a noose considering that Matthew, Victors son, had hung himself.

"I'm sorry, what with Matthew and all," Ben says, "but I don't know how else to tell you. It was pretty damn disturbing to see."

Silence seems to go on forever. Finally, Victor says, "So where did you say this happened?"

"In the garage, our garage. Jimmy came home from school and, well…"

Victor draws in a breath and exhales faintly. He turns to Ben and says, "Okay. See…a couple of months ago someone did the same on my back porch."

"You're kidding," Ben blurts. He's shocked, not to learn about the rope and noose on Victor's porch, Ben had seen it himself. He's shocked to hear that someone other than Victor put it there. All along Ben assumed it was Victor who had laced the noose on his porch—for reasons unknown.

"Yeah. I hadn't been here long, barely a week when it happened. I managed to get the disgusting thing down before anyone saw it." He stops talking, takes a small sip of beer, and says, "Sounds to me like some wacko's on the loose. I've seen this before. Well, haven't seen it firsthand, but heard about it. Read about it when I was doing research, background stuff for one of my novels."

"Not the kind of thing that goes on in the Bluff, though," Ben says. "A little shoplifting over at the Menards now and then, or down at the Tractor Store maybe...that's about it."

"Well, just keep your eyes and ears open, Cedar Bluff or not," Victor warns. "That's my advice."

10

Ben hasn't seen Victor for quite a while though he's pretty sure he's in his house working relentlessly away on his book. Like Ben and Amy, Victor keeps his windows open. The early morning and midday weather is pleasant, sheer delight after the long harsh winter. Ben cherishes these days, all of Minnesota does. They cannot not come too soon and cannot not last long enough. Ben hears Victor putzing around in the backyard, occasionally the sound coming from his open window of his noisy printer ticking out pages. One of those old dot matrix printers, Ben surmises, when he hears it. You'd think with all Victor's money he'd have invested in a fancy laser job by now. Who knows? People are weird. Ben does the same sort of thing at the Shell lots of times, preferring to poke away under the hood rather than hook the engine up to the computer diagnostics.

Making good progress on his book, that's what Ben figures. For an entire week, Victor hasn't made an appearance in the backyard to share a Summit or a Surly. Just as good, Ben thinks. He wants Victor to keep slogging away on his book. Maybe this will be his best work ever.

"Won't that be great, Victor Cartuso knocking out an international best seller right there next door to us," Ben says one morning to Amy.

Then, suddenly, the world in the Bluff comes to a crashing halt. These sorts of things don't happen in the Bluff. Have never happened in the Bluff, not in Ben's memory, not in Amy's memory going all the way back to her childhood.

Three blocks away on Eighth Street, Jet Paulson, a classmate of Jimmy's, nicknamed Jet because of his rocket speed on the ice playing for the high school hockey team, is found swinging from the rafters in his garage, stool tipped over beneath his feet.

It could have been suicide. Or might have been an accidental slip as almost happened to Jimmy. Yes, perhaps, but for one telling detail. Jet's hands were tied tight behind his back. No, this was not suicide! Murder, pure and simple.

Ben and Warren, Ben's employee, hear about it from a customer at the Shell. Ben sits stone-faced in the paunchy rescue chair inside the station. Warren looks out the window in disbelief.

After dinner, one that no one eats much of, Ben goes to the living room. No Minnesota Twins game that night, no visit to the backyard with a cooler of ice and beer. Ben, Amy, and Jimmy follow the local news as reporters repeat the same sound bites and film footage standing in front of the Paulson house.

11

The town of Cedar Bluff reels. St. Olga's Catholic Church holds a requiem for Jet. Memorials are given at the Methodist, Presbyterian, and Episcopal churches, and a half dozen others. Groups assemble to help deal with the mourning. For days, the sun seems sucked from the sky over Cedar Bluff.

Murder of this kind is beyond the scope of the Cedar Bluff police department. A pair of crackerjack detectives come in from Minneapolis. There is hardly a person in town who is not paid a visit from 'Joe Friday' and his sidekick 'Bill Gannon'. Missing only is Friday's TV refrain: "Most people are good while some go bad. That's when I go to work. I carry a badge".

Yet, it is all for nothing.

"Could be an outsider, someone who is long gone," The cop speculates, turning the unsolved case back to the local police.

It takes nearly a week for Ben to muster the desire to spend an evening with a beer out back. He tells himself, not just himself but Amy and Jimmy as well, that it's time for life to return to normal as best as possible. No, it's not a 'shit happens' moment, he tells them—that's far too insensitive for big real-world tragedies. But it's time to move forward just the same.

Throughout the Jet Paulson episode, Ben has heard little from Victor. Only the clicking of the printer that periodically rings out every morning from across the fence. But sure as tinkers have pots, it's not ten minutes after Ben parks himself in the lawn chair before he hears footsteps clomping up the driveway. Victor turns the corner of the house, stops, and looks at Ben, waiting to see if it's a good time for a visit.

Ben signals for Victor to have a seat. Victor's face is filled with gloom, deprived of expression. He doesn't reach immediately for a beer. Rather, he waits for Ben to fetch one from the ice chest and pass it to him. Victor holds the can in front of him for a minute before pulling the top.

"Terrible news about the Paulson kid," he utters. He watches Ben's reaction to see if this is safe territory to tread on. Ben explains that Jet was friends with Jimmy, and that Jet and Jimmy were on the hockey team at school.

"This is the kind of…the sort of garbage you deal with in New York almost daily. The stuff I wanted to get away from," Victor says. "But here in the Bluff, yikes…yikes."

"It never happens," Ben confirms. "Never in all the time we've been here."

"I think the cops, those two flatfoots that were poking around, I think they bungled the whole affair pretty badly."

Ben leans lightly on his elbow, waiting for Victor to explain.

"Well, in my opinion, they didn't get all of the physical evidence. For example, the rope and noose that were on my back porch—"

"When they talked to me, I gave them what I had," Ben says, "the noose someone strung in the garage."

"Well, I would have done the same, but they came by when I was out of town."

Ben tries to recall Victor being gone recently. His best recollection says the clicking of the printer has been nearly non-stop every morning for the past ten days, though he hasn't actually seen Victor throughout it all.

"That's right. They left a note in the mailbox saying they wanted to chat with me. But strange, they never came back."

"Well, you can still give the rope to the police," Ben points out.

"Too late. Got rid of it. Didn't want that morbid thing around."

Something in the explanation seems missing, but Ben doesn't probe Victor on it. They are in Cedar Bluff, after all, and in Cedar Bluff, people are mostly trusting. Though Ben is not a native of the Bluff, it would be hard to know he isn't at this point. Got the walk, got the talk.

"Now here's what I think," Victor says in a tone of authority. "That murder there was a local one…as local as, what's that fish you folks like…local as a walleye. It wasn't done by someone passing through town or whatever theory those two dicks were peddling. Doesn't add up. Cripes, I've spent my whole life writing about this crap. When you do that day in and day out, you get to know the ropes. You become the cop *and* the killer both. You need to be if you're going to write a convincing mystery, something people will believe, something that'll keep them flipping the pages."

"Huh, never quite thought of it that way."

"Oh, yeah. You have to be one step ahead of the cops and one step ahead of the killer all at the same time. If you're not the whole crutchin' story comes to an effing halt pretty darn quick."

"So, you think it's a local job?"

"Course it is. And how many people did you say you have here in the Bluff? Doesn't matter, not very many. Sooner or later the word will leak out. Sooner or later someone will figure out who the whodunnit is. Could be the guy or the kid down the street. Could be one of your regulars over at the Shell. Pretty scary stuff, huh? See, you have to think like a killer to do what I do."

Ben fishes through the ice for a Surly. "Too bad you had to arrive in the Bluff when this crap is happening. Especially after the big shout-out I gave you about how great life is here. Peace and quiet and all that hooey. Hope what happened isn't disturbing your book writing."

Victor takes in a soft breath, as if mildly exasperated, and says, "So far so good. I try to get into the zone and stay with it. If I can do that, I'm okay usually." He takes a small swig of beer and sets the can on the ground beside him. He wants to light a cigarette, but doesn't. The pack in his breast pocket is speaking to him, but it stays unopened.

Ben doesn't care if Victor lights up, especially at a time like this, but he doesn't encourage him either. As for Ben, there's no temptation for a smoke. The breath of the devil is forever gone from his lungs.

12

Cedar Bluff hasn't fully recovered from the death of Jet Paulson. Probably never will.

Ben isn't sure if he should believe Victor when he said someone put a noose on his back porch while he was gone one morning and that he came home and there it was, swinging sweetly in the tranquil summer breeze.

But, of course, that is how it happened in Ben's own garage. Jimmy sure as hell didn't toss the noose over the beam.

And anyway, where would Jimmy get a rope like that? Something they use on the ore boats that chug up and down the Great Lakes. And where would he have learned to make a noose, one good enough to put a smile on a hangman's face?

Ben sinks into the rescue chair at the Shell and thinks. So, who then had access to our garage? Jimmy, Amy, me. That's it. Oh, wait. Didn't I give a key to Warren once? That time we were heading down to Chicago for a week? Warren said he'd give the lawn a whack while we were gone. Yeah, I did leave the key with him. But did I get it back? Huh…not sure.

The memory fogs over when it comes to the little details of life. Those inconsequential matters that don't normally need to be locked away in long-term memory.

Ben thinks hard. Can he picture Warren flipping the key to him at the station when he returned from Chicago? Nope. What about Warren stopping by the house and giving it to Amy? Nope. But that doesn't mean Warren didn't return it. It just means Ben can't recall. And Ben's not about to question his tried-and-true employee, someone who's worked for him for nearly ten years. Virtually insulting him, making it look like he might have intentionally kept the key to do something devious later.

A car pulls up for gas. The bell in the bay rings twice.

"Stay put, I'll get it," Ben calls to Warren.

"Give her a fill…she's running on vapors," Oliver Nagel says. "And if you go past that hood, take a peek at that oil too, will ya? But if you're real busy, you can just let her go."

Ben's known Oliver from back when Ben bought the station.

A song comes from Oliver's radio, one of those moldy-oldy stations: The Grateful Dead, *Ripple*.

Ben hums along as he takes the hose from the pump and inserts it into the tank and starts the gas flowing. He goes around and raises the hood, pulls a shop rag from his pocket and reads the dip stick. He sets the hood down and gives a push till it clicks.

"She's okay," he calls. "Come by next week and we'll change her out just to be on the safe side. Pennzoil...the best. That way you won't need to do it again until mother nature's done beating the bejesus out of us this winter."

"Oh sure, now that's the thing to do, all right," Oliver says.

Ben sets the hose back on the pump. Oliver holds a credit card out the window.

When Ben returns, Oliver says, "So, didja hear? They think they got a lead on the Jet Paulson case."

"Wow, now that's news, all right! What's this all about?"

"Don't know the details, but it's become quite the buzz."

"A suspect?"

"Not even sure of that. You know the cops...hold those cards real close to their chest, they do."

"I'll check with Warren. He's up on everything that happens in the Bluff."

Ben breaks the news to Warren in the bay.

"Heard it just this morning," Warren says, pulling a muffler from a car up on the lift. He stops and looks at Ben. "A local, they're saying. That's what they believe. Someone from right here amongst us. One of our own." He points out the door of the bay with his wrench. "Get a load of that, will ya! Someone from right under our own nose."

"From here in the burg?" Ben says.

"Yeup, from the burg."

Ben circles in a small orb. "Damn," he mumbles. He looks at Warren. "Now what?" he wonders aloud. "Should I tell

Amy? What about you? You gonna mention it to Jennifer?"

"Don't know," Warren says. "Might. Either way, she'll find out soon enough on her own."

Ben shudders. He shakes his head and says, "Amy, too. Probably should tell her, regardless. Not Jimmy. Let him find out from his buddies or whatever. He's having a tough time coping with the death of Jet as it is."

"Say, you don't think this guy's gonna strike again, do ya?" Warren poses.

Ben pretends he hasn't considered the possibility, but of course he has. It's on the mind of every soul in the Bluff.

Later in the afternoon, Victor Cartuso swings his car in for his weekly tank "top off". Afterward, he invites Ben to join him in his backyard for a Surly or a Summit, if he's feeling up to it. "Sucked up too much of your beer not to return the favor, I think," Victor says.

Ben accepts the offer. He doesn't bring up the news about the Jet Paulson killer.

13

The evening is unusually hot and humid, full of air that clings close to the skin. Ben tells Amy he's heading over to Victor's after dinner to share a brew.

Amy thinks it's good that Ben continues to connect with their new neighbor. Despite being a pretty good extrovert, Ben hasn't made many close connections in Cedar Bluff, other than the constant flow of the Jack and Jills that come through the station, and the bunch he jives with every couple of weeks at The Schooner, the tavern over on Fourth Street.

Ben arrives at Victor's right on schedule; Victor is waiting. Everything is as picture-perfect as if on a Hollywood set. Two lawn chairs, simple, brand new. Target or Menards, no doubt. The cooler, too. And perfectly placed between the chairs for an easy flip of the lid.

"Hey, there!" Victor barks, sounding as if Ben hasn't been seen in eons. "Pull up a chair and pop a beer, old buddy. Got both of your favorites here. Ice cold." He lifts the lid of the cooler and displays them to Ben.

Ben settles into a chair and retrieves a Summit.

"How is it…cold enough?" Victor asks.

"Thor's nuts in a tin cup," Ben replies.

"Got it right then," Victor says proudly, letting out one of his raspy-throat laughs.

Ben takes in a long slow slug of beer and emits a solemn grunt. "What a day," he utters. He holds the beer can to his forehead for a second.

"Busy?"

Ben nods. "Course, that's what we want. But I don't know, maybe it's the heat and all. Ever have a day when you feel something isn't right? Just not right?"

"Oh, sure…lots of 'em."

Ben rolls the beer can across his forehead again. "Anyway, how's the writing going?"

Victor doesn't answer right off, but Ben can tell from the look on his face that things are all right—whatever that means for a writer.

"Two months now and I'm nearly half done with the book. Get a load of that, damn good progress even for someone like me who can churn out books fast even in the worst of times. Until recently, that is, like we talked about."

"Back to the horror thing?"

"Horror it is. Odd, isn't it…people like getting shocked out of their freakin' drawers? What's *that* all about?"

This is the first time Ben has brought up the writing with Victor in a long time.

"All things considered, it was a pretty good decision to move to the Bluff," Victor says.

In a perverse sort of way, Ben wonders if Victor has constructed a novel around the Jet Paulson incident. Didn't he once say he gets his ideas from real life?

"Maybe when I'm done with the manuscript, I'll let you look it over. How's that sound? A neutral pair of eyes is always a good thing. Marla used to do that, but right now I'm sort of on my own…before I ship the thing off to my editor is what I mean."

"Geez, that would be spectacular!" Ben says, leaning toward Victor. That pretty much settles it in Ben's mind. There's no way Victor could write about Jet Paulson's death, or even anything close to it, and turn the manuscript over to Ben to read.

The effect of the alcohol works nicely on Ben's tight nerves. He slumps in the chair. "Got some news today about the Paulson thing."

"They got a lead on the killer," Victor says.

Ben squints a look at Victor. "How the hell'd you know that?"

"Whole town knows. This is—"

"Cedar Bluff. You're right. No secrets in the Bluff," Ben says, as if it's more of a problem than a good thing. "Yep, no secrets in the Bluff."

"This is what I predicted," Victor says. "Sooner or later someone'll spill the beans. Even if the perp did it all by himself, killed Paulson is what I mean, someone'll figure it out, will know who did it. A friend, a buddy…someone. See, fact is we're not very good at hiding ourselves from the world. We think we are, oh yeah, we think so, but it's total bullshit. People around us have a better handle on us than we ourselves do."

Ben ponders this for a second. He rolls the can of Summit across his forehead again. "You're right about that, I think. We don't fool anyone very well, do we? Not really?"

Victor rests his chin on his palm as if considering some recondite thought. After a while he says, "Well, anyway, what I've always wanted to do more than anything is write a book about the perfect crime, the perfect murder. Lots of people have done this, but let me tell you, those books make for great reading. The whodunnits that throw you for a total loop at the end."

"You think the Paulson case will end up like that when they finally get the, what did you call him…the perp?" Ben asks.

"Absolutely," Victor replies with total certainty. "Can't end any other way. You'll see."

"What about the leads the cops have?"

"Dead ends, all of them…rabbit holes."

Ben reaches for another Summit.

"Cops here don't know that yet, though," Victor adds. "No detective in New York would get snookered like this. In fact, they'd probably have the perp in the cage by now. The only ones who get away with murder in New York are the pros…the mob, the hitmen. They know all the tricks."

"Now what?" Ben says.

"It's entirely possible the case will solve itself. Someone

drops a tip to the cops, like I just said."

Ben pops the Summit.

"Then, too, you have to consider that Jet's death might not be murder."

"Not murder?"

"That's right."

"What? Suicide?"

"Nope. Kids playing around. A pal ties Jet's hands behind his back and loops the noose around his neck and wraps the rope over the rafters. The kid is up on the stool, see. They're just goofing off…nothing more. But then Jet slips. Takes a nose dive sideways off the stool and, voilà, there he is, twirling in circles by his neck, helpless…turning blue." Victor snaps his fingers. "That fast, it's over. Seeing what happened, Jet's pal freaks and high-tails it fast out of the garage."

"He doesn't tell anyone? Nobody?" Ben says.

"Would you?"

Ben shrugs. "I don't know." He thinks about this; the fear that Jimmy might have been involved fills Ben's thoughts. Jimmy, probably Jet Paulson's closest friend. Jimmy, the one who found the noose in their own garage. What if Jimmy was in Jet's garage showing him what he had found? Maybe they strung a noose up and started screwing around like Victor described. Good Lord, what if it was Jimmy who inadvertently…? The thought sends shivers down Ben's spine.

Time to talk baseball.

14

For several days, at home, at work, everywhere, Ben continually thinks about his conversation with Victor.

If what Victor suggested is true, and it did make sense, there are three possible explanations for Jet Paulson's death. Murder, suicide, accidental death. Of all, the third worries Ben the most because of the possible implications for Jimmy.

It's clear Jimmy is deeply troubled by the death of his friend. He mopes around the house, saying little. Blank stares, emotionless. He doesn't go for the second or third splat of mashed potatoes at dinner. The usual grind of music coming from his room is gone.

Should Ben talk to him, ease his way into the topic and find out how he's feeling? Sometimes, kids just need an opening. Ben knows that from his own childhood. Being a father, he knows it even more. But Ben does nothing. Instead he watches Jimmy meander through the house and head to his bedroom.

Nor does Ben divulge his conversation with Victor to Amy. No point in getting her any more upset than she already is.

Then everything changes. In the morning, a car pulls in for gas. It's Victor. He delivers his usual, "Fill 'er up, old buddy."

Ben tops off the tank.

"Heading out for a couple of days again," Victor says. "Have some business to take care of out that way." He waves his hand, which could mean up in the Cities—Minneapolis and St. Paul—or out west somewhere, or across the river in Wisconsin. "You don't think I can bother you to grab the mail again, do you?"

"You know you can."

Victor holds the house key and a credit card for the gas out the window. When Ben returns, Victor is staring up at the sky as if sizing up the weather. Big white powder puff clouds stroll across the blue ceiling overhead.

"Good day for a road trip," Ben says. He's tempted to ask Victor where he's going. He hands him the card and the receipt. "Anyway, you drive careful now. We have our share of loonies behind the wheel right here in Minnie."

Victor nods compliantly.

Ben returns home at dinner time. He showers, climbs into a set of clean clothes, goes next door, and picks up Victor's mail from the box by the curb. Two bills, electric and water, and something from New York. Official looking with a fancy embossed return address: Carol Grossman Associates. Victor's literary agent, betcha, Ben assumes.

He holds the envelope up, tilting it to see what's inside. Could be a check, but it's hard to tell. Not bad, he thinks, write a bunch of books and the bucks come rolling in.

Ben unlocks the door and goes in. It's pretty much as it was last time he was there. He sets the mail on the dining room table and looks around. The framed article describing Victor's son is no longer on the bureau. Huh, must have moved it, Ben figures. I sure would have. Pretty dreary thing to keep out in full view. Biting you every time you pass by. Not exactly what I'd want to be reminded of day after day. Wonder what he did with it?

Ben's desire to be nosey is growing by the second.

On the opposite side of the table is Victor's laptop. A printer sits on a small table in the corner by the window. Yeup, he tells himself, just as I suspected last time…it's where he grind out the words to his novel every morning, right here on the dining room table.

He looks around the room and goes over to where papers are spread out. The urge to snoop finally wins out. He takes a small stack of ten or twelve pages and turns them over and starts reading. Something about a boy. Seems to be near to Jet Paulson's age, Jimmy's age. A small town. Sounds a hell of a lot like the Bluff. But could easily be anywhere in Minnesota, or the whole stretch of burgs across the northern states.

Ben flips to another page. Some kind of crap is going on, for sure. And it doesn't sound at all good. A kid is dead. "Geez Louise," Ben mutters. Not just dead. Strung up by his neck from a beam in the garage.

Enough okay. Ben rearranges the pages, trying to put them exactly as he found them. Don't need Victor to discover I was snooping through his stuff, huh? That would suck. Victor did say he gets his ideas from real life, now didn't he? Well, there you have it, Ben reassures himself. Can you really blame him? Still, sort of morbid thing to do, to exploit a real-life tragedy. Especially when your own son died that way. Hey, screw it…his business, not mine.

Ben ventures into the kitchen, feeling even more guilty to be doing so, but he knows that's where the door to the basement is. They always put the basement door in the kitchen in these old houses.

For reasons unclear, Ben's instincts take him to the door. Arms folded, he stares at it for quite a while, pondering whether to open it. Should he? More time and more thinking and then he reaches for the knob and gives a humble little twist. It turns easily, but the door doesn't open. Peeking along the edge of the frame, he sees the bolt of the lock.

He smells something. What is it? A unique odor. He knows it but can't place it. Drawing in a deeper breath, he takes a full sample of the air that leaks from the crack. Then it hits him. Formaldehyde, yes. Formaldehyde for sure. The same crap they use in biology class when they give you one of those rubbery bullfrogs to cut open.

He gives the door another gentle tug. "Okay, dude, let's not break the latch," he utters. The last thing he wants is to explain how the lock on the basement door got broken.

Enough…enough of this, get your ass out of here.

Ben leaves and locks the front door. But his curiosity doesn't relent. He circles the house and peers into the half-dozen basement windows hoping for a view. No such luck. All are safely covered with curtains.

Just for the hell of it, he pulls up on a window jamb. No…can't be! The window slides up. On his knees, hands on his hips, staring at the window, he knows it would be easy to climb in. It'd be a snap. But there's no bloody way he's going to do that. None! He pushes the window down and heads home.

For three days, Ben repeats the routine at Victor's house, all but for the skulking around outside. He dutifully picks up the mail, sets it on the table, and leaves.

Victor didn't say when he'd return, but no matter, it's easy to walk fifty feet and collect the mail. Same old mail for the most part—bills and flyers, those damn advertisements that pack the mailboxes. It is what it is. Then, too, another letter from The Carol Grossman Agency, the one with the fancy embossed return address. That makes two in just a couple of days. As before, Ben holds the envelope to the sky and angles it up and down, trying to glimpse its contents. Pretty slick, he considers once again. Park your ass behind a laptop, crank out a bunch of books, watch the bucks roll in. Sure, but somehow it can't be all that easy or every doofus in the world would be doing it.

On the third day after he's done delivering the mail, Ben goes to the unlocked basement window. He gapes at it for a minute, then looks around the yard and at the house across the back fence, the O'Toole place—an old two-story affair that has a straight shot down on Victor's yard. If Ben were to go into the basement, they could easily see him. Maybe even catch a short video from their cell phone. That's what happens in the age when everyone is granted fifteen minutes of irrefutable fame, like it or not. Is it worth the risk? Ben watches the O'Toole's place, no activity from what he can tell. He knows they rarely get home before six o'clock.

Ben wipes his forehead and thinks a second longer. Screw it! He kneels and lifts the window sash. It rises easily for one that probably hasn't budged in years. He slips stealthily into the basement and lowers the window. The basement is dark but Ben knows there must be a light switch somewhere at the top of the stairs.

He feels his way over, grabs the railing, climbs the stairs, and flips the switch. Turning, he scans the musty room. Empty, mostly. That death-smell of formaldehyde is strong. How can Victor tolerate this, he wonders. He walks across the room. Over near the wall is a glass gallon jug of it—thirty-eight percent it says on the label. There is no evidence of what it's used for. No pickled bullfrogs. No ducks with spread-out wings as if caught in mid-flight, no seven-foot grizzlies. In fact, the room is quite empty and orderly.

One of Ben's skill saws is plugged into the wall next to a stack of two-by-fours and four-by fours and half-inch plywood. For no particular reason, Ben picks up the saw. He checks the blade and then sets it down.

There's a thick rope on the floor, wound in a circle in an

old frayed cardboard box, looking like a cobra about to strike. Rope of the kind Jimmy found strung up in their garage.

"Geehosophat!" Ben softly utters, crouching down and taking a close look at the rope.

The work of Victor's carpentry is in the far corner of the room. Not the finest bit of craftsmanship, to be certain, but not the worst either. A boxed-in area made of plain plywood with an off-the-rack door, Menards or Lowe's. A solid door through and through, based on the sound Ben gets when he raps it with a knuckle. So too, Victor has added a hell of a strong hasp with a hell of a large padlock. Little chance of getting inside that baby, Ben concludes, short of taking a fire axe or a ten-pound sledge to it.

There's not much else to see. No huge surprises when you size it all up. Ben looks around one last time, pushes up the window, and squirms out. He looks immediately across at the O'Toole place, feeling suddenly guilty about his Paul Pry act, but from all appearances, he made it out undetected.

□

Ben comes into the station at ten o'clock the next morning. Warren is always there bright and early. Both bays are empty—a car is waiting to be rolled in. Tune-up, according to Warren, with a check of all the fluids, especially the antifreeze. An easy job.

Warren is sitting in the rescue chair working on a Marlboro. These days, he starts with four of them in his shirt pocket.

His ration. His Dr. Pepper approach: Ten, Two, and Four…and one for good measure.

A thin balloon of smoke hovers up near the ceiling. Ben pours a cup of coffee from the Krups and shakes powdered cream into it from a large plastic container.

"How it goes?" Ben asks.

"Oooh, not so bad," Warren replies, which Ben has come to know is Minnesotan for pretty good.

Ben gives his coffee a stir.

"I see your writer fella is back in town," Warren says.

Ben returns a surprised look. "You don't say. When did that happen?"

"Went through a full tank of gas on his trip. That's what he said."

Ben calculates: knowing the make of the car, its age, figuring Victor is no Indy driver, he predicts the trip to be somewhere about two hundred and fifty miles out, two-fifty back. "That covers a lot of ground in wide-open Minnie," he states.

"Ye-uh, you got that one right, okay," Warren says. "You can go all over the place out there even with that twelve gallon bucket he has in that thing." He pulls in the last precious drag from the Marlboro. Smoke curls from his mouth and winds out his nose.

Ben wants to tell Warren what he found at Victor's house: the pages from the book that he's writing, the locked basement door, the formaldehyde, what he saw in the basement. But he knows better than to tell Warren anything unless you want it spread around the entire burg. You never share the important shit with him—Loose Lips Sink Ships.

☐

As per script, Victor shows up at Ben's in the evening for an ice-cold can of Minnesota's finest. It isn't long before he brings up a topic that causes Ben's stomach to grind.

"You wanna hear something real strange?" Victor says.

Ben looks at Victor and waits.

"I came back from the trip and when I went to the basement, guess what I found?"

Oh, Jesus…no! Ben thinks.

"The basement light was on." He gives Ben an uncomfortable, almost accusatorial look, or so it seems to Ben anyway.

Victor takes a small sip of beer and lets it roll through his mouth. He looks toward the sky as though thinking, and says, "Course I can't be one hundred percent certain I didn't do it. Leave the light on is what I mean. Can't be certain I didn't. I was moving pretty fast trying to get on the road early that day. I thought I flipped the switch, but who knows? This memory thing of ours," he taps the side of his head with his finger, "it's not all that reliable, if you want the truth. In fact, one time I had a long conversation about it with a shrink friend of mine. He told me that most of the time what we believe happened is a pretty piss-poor version of the real thing. That's why eyewitnesses in court are so problematic…unless you have a whole pile of them saying the exact same thing."

Ben emits an undetectable sigh of relief.

"But that's not what bugs me…the light being on and all. What bugs me is that some clown got into the basement while I was gone."

"Really," Ben says, sporting his best no shit look. "How do you know that?"

"Easy. Photos."

"Photos?" Ben says in nearly a whisper.

"Yep, photos. This baby may not be so reliable," tapping his head again, "but *this* baby is." He retrieves his phone from his pocket, holds it out, and gives it a couple of shakes for emphasis. "They're all here…right here on this little gadget. Care to see?"

"Course," Ben declares, clearing his throat.

Victor doesn't go to the photos, not immediately. First, he rambles through an iteration about his compulsive habit of periodically snapping pictures inside the house.

"See, when we lived in Gotham, some lowlife got into our place and all but cleaned us out. Laptops—two of them. Couple of cameras. All the high-end crap that's easy to stuff in a sack and walk away with. Well, there wasn't much we could do about it. Gone…gone forever. That much I knew."

"Okay, gotcha," Ben says. He starts for another beer and realizes he has the better part of a full can right there in his hand; he winds his arm over his shoulder pretending to be working a stiff muscle.

Victor shows Ben the photos. "See that, it's the skill saw. Your skill saw. Now look here." He flips to another picture. "Notice the difference. This creep, whoever he is, picked up the saw, checked it out apparently, and set it down again. See how it's been moved?"

Ben looks carefully at the photo. "Definitely." He wonders if Victor is going to do the same with the rope, but Victor says nary a word.

"So, you ask, how did someone get into the basement, right? Window, that's how. The one on the north side was unlocked. My bad."

Ben gives Victor a, sure, that explains it sort of nod.

"So, this creep was down there poking around but didn't lift anything...nothing's missing. Not even the skill saws, which in my book would have pulled in quite a few bucks, even at a flea market somewhere."

Ben chimes in. "*Bucks?* Ho, those babies are not cheap."

15

Then…again.

The news sweeps through Cedar Bluff like a West Texas wildfire. Death by hanging. Sixteen years old. In the garage. This one, however, is not suicide. No prank gone wrong. This is flat out murder.

Ben is at home and about to leave for work. Victor knocks on the door. In a sad and terse voice, he tells Ben what he just learned. Not much in the way of details yet. Another kid, dead, hanged. Too hard for Victor to discuss on such a beautiful summer morning. His eyes moisten over as he turns and walks away. There's a look on Victor's face that Ben's never seen before, one that says, how the hell did I end up in a place caught in the talons of a serial killer?

Amy is sitting at the kitchen table, face in her hands, too shocked to cry. She heard the news moments ago from a friend who called.

She looks at Ben, says nothing. Ben sits in a chair, slowly, as if it will give way under his weight. He can't look at Amy. The silence is bone chilling.

Finally, he says, "Going to work. Shutting it down for the day." He gets up and leaves.

Warren is standing with his hands in his pockets staring stone-faced out the window, eyes locked onto some far-off sight. Ben tells him he's closing up. Warren nods.

The day is as warm and blissful as any that came to Cedar Bluff, but the news has turned it bleak and cold.

Warren starts to say something, stops, shakes his head and leaves.

Ben sets the CLOSED sign in the window and locks up. He knows he should go home and be there for Amy and for Jimmy when he arrives, but he needs a moment alone.

He drives over to Bluff Lake and sits on a bench and watches the mist rise and dissolve off the water—the flat surface of the lake now and then broken by the tail of a pumpkinseed or a crappie. For one quick moment, Ben hates Cedar Bluff, not that what happened is the town's fault. Yet the anger that rises in him turns into resentment.

Two people sit at a bench off to Ben's right. A man farther down is hunched, inert as a stone statue.

When Ben returns home, Amy is at the kitchen table looking as if she hasn't moved a muscle. "Amanda Lund," is all she says.

Ben stops in the kitchen doorway as he processes the information. "Amanda Lund," he repeats. Then it hits. "You can't be serious," he mutters.

Amy nods. "Same thing as Jet Paulson...garage and rope."

A chill runs through Ben.

A girl, a teenager. Amanda Lund. Part of Jimmy's high school clique, as Ben fondly calls it. All nice kids. All happy kids. Lucky kids. Kids without a worry.

There's Augustino—Tino to Jimmy and his buddies—from the Hispanic family that came to Cedar Bluff from Milwaukee. His father owns a roofing company. You see the white van around town. The one with the ladders on top and an image of a smiling house painted on the side. And there's Bobby, the only non-jock in the bunch. A nerd, to be sure. Nerdy and funny, with a grin that fills his face like that on large-mouth bass, a hee-haw laugh that's a gas to hear. And Toby Milton, the smartest kid in Jimmy's class, destined for Harvard or Yale or Princeton, Hopkins maybe—the boyfriend of Amanda Lund.

Mr. Lund is a doctor, family practice. He went to medical school at the University of Minnesota but set his sights on work in a small town.

Mornings and afternoons trolling for a good catch with a spoon is his idea of how to spend his day off, not out making the rounds on the links. He has two kids. Amanda is the raving beauty, the oldest. Nobody could dislike Amanda. A smile as clean as glacial water, blue eyes donated to her by her Scandinavian genes. Ben knows the Lunds well. They come to him religiously for gas and repairs.

What's going on, Ben wonders, worries. It's like Jimmy's

group is being picked off one by one by some strange mafia hitman.

How many times has Jimmy and his bunch come storming through the house and out to the backyard to shoot hoops? Or play baseball together in the park? Or skate on one of the lakes in the winter? And now Jet Paulson and Amanda Lund, two of the group, are gone. Never again will they crash through the front door with the others heading for the backyard.

"Amanda Lund," Ben repeats once more, his voice quavering, fists squeezed. "Where's Jimmy?" he asks tremulously.

"With his friends," Amy replies.

Ben starts to get up.

"Let him go," Amy says, grabbing Ben's arm. "Let him go. He'll be here when he's ready.

Ben sits down. "Makes you want to go out all by yourself and find the fucker that's doing this," Ben says. "The killer. This is little Cedar Bluff, for Christ's sake. How hard can it be to find the guy in a place like this? How hard can it be? How the hell hard can it be?"

"They will, they will. They always do…well…don't they?"

Ben tells Amy what's been gnawing at him for weeks, though he hasn't mentioned it to her. About how all the bad stuff in the burg began right after Victor Cartuso arrived, even going so far as to tell her about what Victor's writing, the novel he's working on. The kid being hanged and all.

"Now, Ben!" Amy says. "I know you're upset. My God,

we're all upset. But let's not go and start blaming our neigh-bors, no matter who they are. I don't care if they just got here soon or not. Victor's a perfectly fine person…okay? Kind and gentle and decent."

"But isn't that what always happens, when they finally get the sleaze, the killer, I mean? It's always someone who…"

"Stop it now!"

"You can't say he *didn't* do it."

"And you can't say he *did*."

16

Once more, Cedar Bluff reels.

Supermarket lines are silent. No chatter, no guffawing with the person behind you or in front of you. It's as quiet as a morning of bass fishing on the lake…with none of the joy. The town pulls into a cocoon of fear.

Little by little the details of what happened begin to emerge. Some of it in the newspaper. Most of it just hearsay passed from person to person. From a cop to a friend to another friend, down the human grapevine of information. But as usually happens, it's hard to know what's accurate and what's not. Versions vary widely. Yet, some themes hold up.

Amanda Lund came home from school alone. Evelyn Garbo, the next-door neighbor, saw her unlock the front door and go inside. Probably three forty-five is what Evelyn told the police when they interviewed her.

What she didn't say is that she heard Amanda in her bedroom. Lots of noise. Lots of moaning. Just like when she was getting banged by Toby Milton—the quickies they had nearly every day after school before Amanda's parents showed up.

But on that day, Evelyn Garbo never saw Toby Milton arrive. And you can be sure she would know it if he had, being the inquisitive biddy she is. In fact, she kept a running tally of Amanda's daily, weekly, monthly bedroom escapades, all recorded in a neat leather-bound book—dates, times, whom Amanda was with. And next to each entry were the letters FBO, Evelyn Garbo's abbreviation for Fucked Brains Out.

It was easy for Evelyn to hear it so long as she plastered her ear against the wooden fence that separates the Lund and Garbo properties. The old houses in Cedar Bluff were platted close together dating to the days when your neighbor was almost part of your own family, a near necessity during the terribly long and treacherous frozen winter months.

For nearly a year Toby Milton had been Amanda's conquistador during their daily afternoon adventures. Amanda was ever faithful to him, and he to her. In the old days, she would have worn his ring on a gold necklace. But that corny tradition hasn't been seen since Amanda's parents were her age.

Based on the entry in Evelyn Garbo's book, Amanda's fateful day was little different from any other, all but for one significant variation. Amanda had come home alone. No Toby Milton. Of that, Evelyn Garbo was certain, given the attention with which she followed every episode of Amanda's life. As faithfully as some people watch Oprah every day, for example. Garbo's notebook recorded Amanda's after school frolics down to the minute, damn near the second.

And so, what really did happen that day, Evelyn Garbo wonders. Was the FBO she had entered next to the date a mistake? Was something sinister, something nefarious, going on that afternoon?

All of Evelyn's information about Amanda is irrelevant now, however. It will never make its way into the hands of the police because soon after Evelyn heard about Amanda's death, she built a roaring fire in the fireplace, tossed the book in, and watched as each page turned to thin black ash one by one. She was not about to find herself in the Cedar Bluff Police Station explaining the origins and purpose of the book.

17

With great reluctance, Ben opens the station two days later. He can't keep it closed forever. The Bluff needs Ben and Ben needs the Bluff. Other stores begin to open one by one.

People grant their neighbors a nod and a trifle smile and then go about their business. Warren says little as he moves routinely and slowly about the bay, stopping more frequently than usual for a visit to the rescue chair, gazing and thinking.

Thursday morning, a Cedar Bluff police cruiser pulls to the pump. Officer Todd Richards steps officiously out of the car. Ben goes to the pump.

"We're fine," Richards tells Ben. "Filled her up yesterday."

Ben is hoping for information about Amanda Lund, but he lets Richards take the lead.

"Need to have you come with me…down to the station for

a minute…can you make it?" Richards says.

"Now?"

"That's right."

"Well, sure, of course." Ben tells Warren he'll be back in a while.

Warren rubs his hands on a rag. "What's Richards up to?"

Ben shrugs. He goes out and climbs into the police cruiser and leaves with Richards.

At the station, Richards leads Ben to the locked police evidence room. On the table is a box. Ben recognizes it instantly—the same dusty cardboard box he saw on the floor in Victor's basement. If it's not the same one, it sure as hell looks like it. More to the point, coiled inside is a winding of rope just as in Victor's basement.

"Got a few questions to ask," Richards says, straight, direct, no apology in his voice.

"Shoot."

"Ever see this thing?" Richards points at the box and the rope.

Geez, now what, Ben wonders. Should he answer? Ben squints as he tries to dig up a reply appropriate for Richard's question. Christ, where the hell did Richards get this thing? Not from Victor Cartuso, Ben hopes.

"Boy, big rope, that much I can say. Remember, we gave you folks one just like this, the time not long ago when Jimmy came home and found it strung up in our garage…back before all the…before the stuff…you know."

Richards nods. "But this rope here is the one I'm interested in."

"Where'd it come from?" Ben asks.

"In a minute." Richards puts on a pair of surgical gloves and tilts the box up, revealing a faded label with Ben's name and address typed on it. Not his house address but the address of the Shell station.

Ben straightens up. He looks menacingly at Richards. "This isn't mine…surely you don't think—"

"Not thinking anything special right now, Ben. Just showing you what we got. Trying to fit some pieces together."

"Where'd it come from?" Ben asks again.

"Front of the police station. It was on the steps when Bobby came in this morning."

Ben crosses his arms defiantly. "Todd, I've known you for years. You don't *really* believe that thing is mine, do you? You *can't* believe that."

"Don't know what to believe quite yet. Except that someone left it with us. And it looks ominously like the one used on Jet Paulson and Amanda Lund. Can't say for sure, but we're having it tested."

"Well, test on."

"Take it easy. No one's saying it's yours, Ben. Just showing you what we have."

"Mind if I take a closer look?"

"If you need to. But put these on first." He hands Ben a pair of gloves.

Ben slips them on as adroitly as a TV doc about to head

into the OR. He tilts the box on its side and inspects the label.

"Just a look. Don't mess with her," Richards says.

Ben bends over and zeroes in on the label.

"Your address at the station…right?" Richards says.

Ben grunts a reply.

"You ever use rope like that?"

"Oh…could. You know, pulling some jalopy out of a snowbank or something, I suppose. Can't say I remember doing that, though. Mostly we use the wrecker."

"Still need one thing, Ben. And I do hate to ask, but…well…we need you to give us fingerprints. This box is loaded with them and…you get the picture."

Ben breathes deeply, groans and nods.

□

The visit to the police station sends Ben into a tailspin. The suggestion that he, one of the Bluff's most trusted citizens, could be linked to the physical evidence of the murders, tears him to pieces. He's far too upset to work. He tells Warren he's taking the afternoon off. Warren wonders what's the deal with Todd Richards, but he doesn't ask.

Ben again sits for hours on a bench down at Cedar Lake watching the birds on the shore, two lone boats out on the lake each with a lone fisherman. The sky is clear; the day should be wonderful.

That night at dinner, Ben wears a smile that looks so artificial Amy asks if there's a problem.

18

Ben sits near catatonic and watches the Twins game, barely paying attention to it.

The phone rings. "It's for you, hon. Victor, from next door," Amy says.

Ben takes the phone. "Vic, what's up?" Ben says, with little enthusiasm.

"Sorry to bother you but…got some time tonight?"

"Tonight? Uh-huh."

"Where's a good place to talk…to go have a drink maybe."

"The Schooner over on Fourth Street, I suppose. Good as any."

"The Schooner it is. In half an hour say?"

Ben goes upstairs and changes his shirt and comes down and tells Amy he's meeting Victor for a drink.

"So, what's up with Victor?" she asks.

"Don't know. Sounds sort of glum," Ben says, buttoning

his shirt. "But then you can't predict Victor. Some days he's floating high, the next time he's practically crawling on the ground. Up and down, that's Victor Cartuso. Pert near bipolar when you come right down to it."

"Oh, let's not get psychiatrist on him now, okay hon? I heard that's how people from New York are."

"Well, he's not from New York actually. But no matter…I'm gone."

He pecks Amy a kiss, retrieves his keys from the kitchen counter, drives the few short blocks to The Schooner, parks in the side lot, and walks into the tavern. Compared to the bright light of the northern evening sky, The Schooner seems dark as a tomb. Ben stands in the entrance for a second letting his vision come to terms with the flat tavern light.

"Ben, hey Ben…over here," Victor calls.

Ben follows the words to a table near the edge of the room. Along the way, he nods at Harold, the bartender, and shoots a nod to Sybil, the waitress. He pulls up a chair at Victor's table.

"Thinking of scotch, for a change," Victor blandly says. "Okay for you?"

"Oh cripes," Ben utters. "I could sure use one of those." He waves to Sybil. "You order," he tells Victor. "I have a pretty good idea you know your scotch."

Sybil comes by, chats with Ben for a second, and says, "So, what'll it be, boys?"

"Couple of single malts," Victor says. "Macallan, perhaps?"

"Water? Rocks? Neat?"

Victor looks at Ben. "Rocks?"

When the scotch arrives, Ben picks up the glass and whiffs the musty aroma. "Lord…I haven't had one of these honeys in a long, long while. Nice break from the beers, huh?"

Victor swirls the cubes in his glass and takes a sip. His jowls, more loose than usual, and his down-turned eyebrows foretell of worries. Ben wonders if he should ask what's going on, but he decides to wait—he'll find out soon enough.

Victor moans. He takes a small hit of scotch, rolls it in his mouth, swallows, and stretches his cheeks wide. He looks intently around the room, though not appearing to pay attention to much of anything, then leans on the table and gives his head a tilt and looks at Ben. "I know what's going on with the murders," he says in a quiet but heavy voice.

Ben sits rock straight, hand on his glass of scotch. Whatever Victor is about to say, it's coming on the heels of Ben's momentously bad day at the police station. On the short drive to The Schooner, Ben all but made up his mind to query Victor about the box with the rope that Todd Richards confronted Ben with. There had to be a way to ask Victor without letting on that he, Ben, had been snooping around in his basement, and admitting that he saw the rope there in the greasy box. But for now, better to see where Victor is headed.

Victor sighs, twice, heavily—deeply and broodingly.

"The murders?" Ben says. "You know who?"

"Yes…I do" Victor says. "I'm going to tell you something, but you don't have to believe me. You don't have to believe a word of it. Just…well…" He stops talking for a moment, then says, "Augh…remember I told you about the tragedy with my son back in Columbus? The thing with the…you know what I'm talking about…the—"

Ben nods promptly to keep Victor from having to relive the sordid details of his son's death.

"Well, what happened was one night back then we had a visitor…a strange man. I have no idea who he was or where he came from. It was eerie, damn eerie…creepy…sickly. My wife and I were asleep upstairs, my son was up in his room. So, I heard a noise and went downstairs. There he was, this person, sitting in the living room. Sort of lean, dressed in black head to foot. Black suit, black shirt, no tie. He had straight black hair that was pulled back. And he had on this black coat like seamen used to wear. It had a tall collar that was pulled up. You've seen them."

"Yeah, yeah, sure."

"He sat in the living room. He was humming a song of some kind. I'm not sure what exactly, but he was humming something almost peaceful. I tried to confront him, to order him out of the house. I threatened him. Said I'd call the police if he didn't leave instantly. He just sat there, totally unfazed. He told me to sit down, more like ordered me to. I almost felt under his control. I sat in a chair."

"Now, you're saying some guy came into your house at night and you don't know who he was and—"

"Yes, that's right. And he told me to listen…listen very, very carefully is what he said. It was totally creepy. I mean, his fingernails came to sharp points at the tips. I remember seeing that. They were either long and filed that way, or that's how they were naturally. And his eyes, Christ, they were like black agates…pure black. He was sitting in one of the chairs, moonlight from outside came in the window and shined directly on him. You could see his face and his features. He had a straight nose and thin lips and sort of high cheek bones, and his cheeks were kind of caved-in as I recall."

Victor stops talking. He takes several repeated sips of scotch and stares into his glass after each one. People passing the table give Ben a tap. He knows them all and they know him—Ben with the Shell station.

Sybil enquires about another scotch; Victor orders a round.

"At first I thought this guy was some fruitcake who managed to get into the house, and that he was playing some kind of sick game with me." Victor swirls the last drop of scotch in his glass, finishes it off, and lets out a low tragic moan.

Ben listens, He wonders if for some odd reason, Victor has spun the whole wild story, maybe just to catch Ben's reaction. When you come right down to it, the guy is a storyteller. Could it be he's spinning the damn thing to see how I'll take it, and then he'll tell me it's all BS. Maybe it's what writers do. How else do they know if an idea works, especially one this bizarre?

"Then came the bombshell," Victor says, his usually rosy face now a dull gray in the sour tavern light. "The man says he has a proposition. I can take it or leave it. It's a yes or no deal.

There are no alternatives…just take it or leave it." Victor's face is aplomb, his jaw almost rigid as he speaks. He stops momentarily, then proceeds. "He, this man, told me the proposition is that he is there to take either Marla, my wife, or Matthew, my son." Victor stops speaking. His eyes begin to float in tears. Blinking several times, he continues, "That's what he told me…Marla or Matthew."

"I'm lost," Ben says. "Take? Take them where?"

"He didn't say. They would go with him, one of them. That's all he said."

"And that you had to say which?"

"That's right."

Ben leans back from the table and shakes his head. "This is preposterous, Victor. How can someone say they're going to take your family from you. It's preposterous."

"I know, I know…I know."

"How would this happen?"

"He didn't explain, except to say that one of them must go with him. He said it didn't matter which one. But one had to go."

"Fuck that," Ben says.

"He added another layer to his proposition," Victor says. "He told me if I didn't decide, he would decide for me, like I just said, but that there would be retribution for my indecision. He never told me what it would be except to say that he had his hand in Fate in many different ways."

Ben is aghast. He sits, stares, listens. "Now you're actually saying a man came into your house and told you he was going to take a person, a member of your family, from you? Just like that?" Ben shakes his head. "Nobody can do that."

"That's what he said," Victor repeats.

"Good God, who was this guy?"

"Someone evil. Some *thing* evil. I don't know who or what he was, but he was not human. That I know now...evilness through and through."

"This is incredible," Ben says, shoulders slumped. "What happened?"

"I was livid. I got up to throw the bastard out of the house, but he merely stood up and held his palm toward me. I was stopped in my tracks, unable to move. He walked calmly to the door. When he got there, he turned. "You had better heed me," he said. "Those words are inscribed in my memory. He said I had forty-eight hours to decide, not a single second longer. That he would get back to me for my answer. And then he did something phenomenal. He held his hand in the air and snapped his fingers. Flames burned from his fingertips."

Ben pulls back and gives Victor a sidelong stare.

"The flames burned for a while and then he snapped his fingers a second time and the flames went out. He proceeded out of the house, humming exactly as he had in the beginning.

"Yeow," Ben stammers. A feeling of pure exhaustion passes through him just from listening to Victor. The Schooner, Ben's occasional place of safety and retreat after a ten-hour day, feels sad and dour. He wonders if Victor's story is to be believed, but he can't imagine him concocting such a terrible tale even for the sake of his writing. He wants to ask Victor what his decision was, but he doesn't have to.

"Forty-eight hours came and went. I found a message in the pocket of my pants. It said: Your decision please. Write it here on the paper. I will find it.

Ben sees Victor's hands tremble.

"My decision? Of course, there was no decision to make. How can you decide between your wife, your soulmate, and your son, the light of your life? *How?*"

Ben slowly shakes his head.

"And this sick creature did exactly what he said he would," Victor says in the most remorseful voice. There is a long grim silence as Victor regains his composure. "It's only recently I've been able to talk about it. I was defiant about the option he gave me, so I did nothing, I did not decide. I never heard from the man again. But everything happened just as he said it would. Two days later, I came home to find Matthew hanging by his neck in the garage. I went crazy. I was screaming, crying, going nuts. But that wasn't all. On that very same day, Marla died also. She was driving down the interstate not far from the house when the front right wheel of her car broke loose. The car went over a guard rail into a ditch. She was pronounced dead on the scene." Victor is speaking quickly, succinctly, as if he needs to get through the story, to finish it, to flesh out the details, and be done with it. He gasps and moans and stares at Ben, hollow and empty. The yellow light of the tavern blots the life from his face.

"Jesus Christ, that's horrendous," Ben utters.

"The police thought there might have been some kind of

hanky-panky related to Matthews death. I knew better, of course. Everything happened exactly as detailed by him, the devil. That's what he was, the devil himself." Victor rubs his brow for a moment, then looks across at Ben. "I've never really recovered. Oh, I managed to get back to work…sort of, I guess you could say I have. But after a while I needed to get out of Columbus, away from New York. Don't ask me how I picked Cedar Bluff. Sounded like a good place to live, I suppose."

"And this man, this person, the visitor, have you ever heard from him again?" Ben asks.

Victor shakes his head. "No…not until now, that is."

"Oh? Meaning what?"

"Meaning, he's here. Right here in Cedar Bluff." Victor taps lightly on the table. "He's the one doing the killings…the kids. At first, I didn't connect the dots. Sure, Jet Paulson was hanged, but then lots of people are hanged—accidently, sometimes suicide. But after the second one, Amanda Lund, then it clicked, then I saw the connection, and then I knew what was going on."

Ben's face is gaunt and lifeless.

"He's here," Victor says. "The devil has *come* to Cedar Bluff. It's real!"

"I don't know, I have trouble believing it," Ben says quickly, almost defiantly. "There are lots of other explanations. Lots."

"Give me one."

"Serial killer of some kind."

"What's going on in Cedar Bluff is not the action of a se-rial killer. I spent my whole life studying those creeps. I know every twist and turn that goes on in a serial killer's mind. I needed to know to make the characters in my books believa-ble."

"All right, but what's he want from us, then? This…who-ever, whatever he is."

Victor shrugs limply. "He will want exactly what he wanted from me. Cedar Bluff will find out soon enough."

Ben looks away in disbelief. How can anything like this happen in quiet little Cedar Bluff, he wonders.

19

Ben returns home weak in the knees from hearing Victor's chilling story. He slumps in a chair and merely tells Amy he had a scotch with Victor at The Schooner , but says no more. Cedar Bluff is already filled with fear and paranoia, no need to fan the flames with wild stories of the likes Ben heard from Victor.

Yet, he is compelled to believe some of it. Ben knows, for example, that Victor's son was hanged. He read the short article from the Columbus newspaper in Victor's dining room. And he knows Marla is dead, though until now he didn't know how she died.

Had Victor concocted a set of bizarre stories to help him deal with both of those calamitous events? People are known to do such things when the soul is deeply troubled. When the psyche is so burdened it can take no more. To rub away the residue of the sorrow, possibly even to rid any lingering guilt, justly or not, that persists.

St. Olga's Church says a requiem for Amanda Lund. The pews are filled, people are standing in the vestibule, a line stretches out onto the steps.

Little by little the town returns to itself.

Ben gets a second visit from Todd Richards. Yes, as predicted, the box with the rope is covered with Ben's fingerprints.

Todd says as far as he's concerned that part of the investigation is closed for now. Which is not to mean Ben is off the hook. Just that they have no compelling reason to continue to suspect him.

But Todd, even being the small-town cop he is, knows that killers come in many forms. Some are even the local Joe you bend an elbow with down at the tavern…or maybe the guy who gasses up your car. He's read enough detective novels to know it.

Ben continues to fret over the origin of the box and the rope. He never puts the question to Victor, though after returning from the police station, he brings the matter up with Warren.

Warren recalls buying a rope some time ago. Says they were thinking of throwing it in the back of the wrecker in case they needed it if the wench went out, but they got a set of big chains instead.

Ben has no memory of this, though he trusts Warren, whose recollection of things is always perfect. Warren says he hasn't seen the rope in quite a while. It somehow disappeared. "Could have been tossed out by mistake, or borrowed it to someone maybe, and they never got it back," Warren says, speaking Minnesotan to mean they lent it.

After a couple of days of stewing about his call into the police station, Ben decides to do something risky. In the morning before going to work, he watches Victor's place, waiting for him to leave. No such luck for three days. Then on the fourth day, Victor pulls out of his driveway a few minutes after nine.

While Amy is up in the shower, Ben trots over to Victors place. Is there any chance the basement window is unlocked?

He goes up the yard to the side of Victor's house, looks quickly at the O'Toole place, and tugs on the window. "Christ," he stammers. The window lifts easily, just like before.

Ben climbs inside. This is stupid, he thinks. Real fucking stupid. What if Victor has set up a security camera? I'll get my ass nailed for sure. As if I'm not already in enough trouble with the cops. But he can't stop, he has to find out.

He moves fast over to the light switch, flips it, and scans the room. Everything is as it was. Well…not quite everything. The skill saw is on the floor precisely as on Ben's first visit— in almost the same position, in fact, as when Victor snapped a photo of it with his phone. But the box with the rope is gone. Could be Victor moved it. The thought worries him. Could be. Or he got rid of it, what with all that's going on these days. Or…huh…or maybe he deposited it on the steps of the police station late at night. Huh…maybe.

That's all Ben wants to know. He turns off the light and is fast out of the basement—and not a second too soon. He hears

Victor's car pull into the driveway. Ben's only exit now is over the fence into his backyard. He pulls himself up and rolls across, hitting the ground and sucking in a deep breath. "Shit, that was *way* too close," he whispers.

He goes into the kitchen from the back door and calls up to Amy. "Hey, love, heading out."

"Coming home for lunch?"

"Not sure. Might go to the diner. Quick and easy."

"See you tonight."

"Love ya."

The conversation with Victor at The Schooner continues to cycle through in Ben's thoughts. Should he believe Victor? He's a hell of a nice guy, a damn good novelist. But is he a total loon? Borderline psycho? What if none of what he said is to be believed: the stuff about his son, about his wife, the visitor late at night? He is a writer and everything he says could be pure fiction.

Or…or what if everything Victor says is perfectly true? Suppose he's connected the dots about the murders in the Bluff the way no one else has. That his assessment, ghastly as it is, is dead right, to use a demented phrase.

Could there be a true evilness lurking in the Bluff that no one could ever imagine?

20

Nothing unusual happens for quite a while. Even Jimmy gradually begins to come out of his shell. Two splats of mashed potatoes at dinner, occasional visits out back to shoot hoops.

They say kids have more resilience than adults. It might be true. Adults have lived long enough to know that even when life finally takes a turn for the better, it doesn't mean it won't slip back into dark territory again. Most kids are naïve enough to believe life is linear—that once past the bad shit, all will be fine. For a period of time early in life we are granted the luxury of that illusion.

Ben isn't at work more than a minute when Warren comes in from the bay. He looks squarely at Ben and says, "Did you hear, Franny Bauer's gone missing?"

"Franny? Walter's wife?"

Warren gives a nod. "Franny. You know Franny. In here every two weeks with that rattle-trap Toyota of hers, the faded blue one. Never drives it in the winter. Stuffs it in the garage and brings it out when the snow and ice are gone. That's the Franny I'm talking about. Heard it a while ago. The story is that Walt came down to the kitchen in the morning, Franny's coffee cup was on the table, half empty, still warm even. But no Franny. Oh ye-uh, I'm saying she was totally disappeared. That's the story I got."

Ben slumps awkwardly in the rescue chair and listens as Warren pours out the details.

"It actually happened yesterday," he says. "Not hide nor hair since. And, boy, you can be sure old Walt is going berserk. You know Franny and Walt, they're like this." Warren holds his hand out and crosses two fingers. "All the way back to high school."

"What about Marty, their son?"

"Marty? Oh, he's fine. Well, upset as hell of course, just like Walt. It so happens that Marty was in town for a short visit. He's going to college up at UMD…you know, Minnesota, Duluth. He landed a job on the docks for the summer. Good job for a kid his age."

"Pretty hard to disappear in a place small as the Bluff," Ben says, shaking his head.

"Cops thought maybe Franny got herself confused and wandered out…got in her Toyota and drove off. They were going to put out a gray alert, or blue alert, or whatever they're called, until they found out that Franny is sharp as a tack. Don't I wish I was that sharp. Besides, the Toyota was still in the garage."

Ben stares out the window.

In the most down voice, Warren says, "Do you get the idea there's a lot of really weird junk going on in the burg? I'm not talking about the deaths of Jet Paulson and Amanda Lund. That's not weird…it's flat out deranged. I mean Franny Bauer disappearing just like that." Warren snaps his fingers. "And while we're at it, have you seen that guy—the tall thin one, the one dressed all in black?"

Ben makes a quick turn to Warren.

"He came in here yesterday while you were at the diner. I had my back to the entrance of the bay. I glanced behind me and there he was staring at me. Just staring. Something ice cold about that look of his. He had his hands in his coat pockets, like he was hiding something. I asked him if he was new to Cedar Bluff and asked if we could help, do some work on his car or whatever. I was just trying to be friendly. He didn't answer. I don't think he had a car, not far as I could tell. He just stood there and stared. It was bothering me…oh ye-uh. And those hands in his pockets. Don't know what that was all about. It was almost as if he had a gun and was about to hold me up. But I knew he wasn't here for that. He was no common criminal. That you could tell looking at him. He asked me if this is Ben Malone's Shell station…your Shell station."

Ben's fingers tighten onto the arm rests of the chair.

"I told him he was right, it is your station. I said you went for lunch and would be back soon. Then he said the strangest thing. Out of the blue, he said he needs a rope. He wanted to know if we might have one."

"A rope…a rope?"

"Before I could answer, he pulls his hand from his pocket and gives a wave, like he's dismissing the whole matter. That's when I saw his fingertips. They were long and pointed. Oh boy, let me tell you, that did it for me. I wanted him outta here."

"You're sure, about his fingers…."

"It happened fast, because he curled them up and slipped them into his pocket again. But I'm pretty certain that's what I saw. He walked off down the street and around the corner."

"Geez Louise," Ben groans. "This was yesterday?"

"Round noon. I meant to mention it but got a flood of cars in here all at once. Five, in fact. I pulled two into the bay and parked three outside. Remember?"

Ben nods.

Warren walks over to the window and looks out. "I guess it's that kind of weirdness I'm talking about. Odd weirdness. The kind we don't usually see in the burg. Or maybe I'm making too much of it."

A car pulls up to the pump. Ben gets up and walks methodically out of the station.

Warren is still looking out the window when Ben returns. He tells Ben what's in line for the day, then says, "Now, you don't think this fella, the one I just described, you don't think he's somehow tied to the murders, do you?" Before Ben can answer, Warren says, "See, that's what weirdness does to you. You start conjuring up all kind of nonsense. Course he did ask about a rope. That was downright strange. Guess I'm trying to fit too many pieces together. Sure would like to see the killer get nabbed."

"About this man," Ben says, "was he wearing a coat? One of those...

"Oooh ye-uh, that's something I forgot to mention. He had on a seaman's coat, black, with the collar turned up. And his hair was pulled straight back over his head and tied in a pony-tail. I remember noticing it when he turned to leave. Hair as black as his clothes."

21

Weeks pass since Ben met Victor at The Schooner. Ben's been avoiding the backyard for his evening beers. Victor, too, is keeping a low profile. Once or twice Ben hears him out back but mostly he's holed up inside. Probably getting close to the end of the book, Ben figures. Oddly, the horrendous news Victor shared at The Schooner doesn't seem to have slowed him down much. That's what Ben surmises, anyway.

When twilight settles in, Ben sneaks out back with a cold can in his hand and he parks himself in a chair. He slumps down, extends his legs, and looks at the sky as it takes on a purple hue that is slowly fading into gray-black.

Ben wanders back to his days as a child growing up in Chicago, all the things he misses that he once took for granted. Afternoons watching the Cubbies. Exhibits at the Art Institute. Concerts in Grant Park. Sneaking into the north side blues clubs as a teenager...oh, the blues! The Blackhawks at the Madhouse on Madison. But, of course, there was the crime. And the traffic. And the snow and ice and cold, which, in fact, he did not escape from when he moved to Minnesota.

His mind sweeps forward to the present. The murders, are they over? Like everyone in Cedar Bluff, Ben worries. The situation Victor related at The Schooner and the person who came to the Shell certainly doesn't alleviate his fears any. Does this degenerate have Ben's family in his crosshairs?

He gets up, goes to the kitchen, and procures another beer from the refrigerator, being careful not to slam the screen door on his way out. Sitting in the chair again, he comes to a terrifying conclusion, one he's been trying hard to avoid. One by one, Jimmy's group is being picked off. Who will be next? Will it be Jimmy? Not if Ben has anything to say about it.

Well into his third beer, Ben makes a decision. If he's paid an unwanted visit late at night, he will be ready. He lays out a plan, a strategy—something stalwart he can go to immediately at just the right moment. "The devil is in the details," he drolls, using a sick analogy. "Oh, yes, the devil is in the goddamn details...and I will have the details nailed down for that SOB!"

Tilting back in the chair, he watches the inky sky speckled with silver stars spread copiously across it.

☐

Night after night, Ben sleeps in fitful spurts, rarely more than an hour at a stretch.

"You've been quite restless these nights," Amy says one morning. "Is everything okay? Something over at the Shell maybe?"

Ben assures her all is fine—just one of those phases.

"Been thinking a lot about Jimmy, I guess. Soon, he'll be heading off to college. Just want to make sure we're ready when he goes. You know, make sure we have enough money to cover it. We've talked about it in the past...but I still worry."

"He's thinking pretty hard about Minnesota over at Mankato. He likes the size of the place. And we know he's waiting to see about that hockey scholarship they keep waving in front of him. Boy now, wouldn't that be nice! Him going to school and playing hockey, which he loves. And getting paid for it, too." Amy pours a cup of coffee. "Course, he'd have to keep his grades up, that's for sure!"

Ben reaches for a mug from the shelf. "You're right. I shouldn't fuss so much about it," he says, pretending it's what's been keeping him awake.

"In fact, Thursday and Friday Jimmy and I are going over there to Mankato to take a look around," Amy says. "Would be awful nice if you could come, but I know you can't get away right now. We'll make another trip later. You can come then."

22

Thursday night arrives. Ben sits in the living room. The house is as quiet as a mausoleum. No Jimmy clomping around. No throbbing music blaring from his room. No endless phone conversations as he paces from room to room.

Ben turns on the TV and grabs a Netflix: *Bourne* something or other. He watches without paying much attention. By ten o'clock, the TV is off and he's in bed. For the first time in days, he falls asleep quickly, barely moving a muscle until late at night when he awakens. The red digital numbers on the clock next to him read just past three a.m. A heavy rain is falling outside, pounding hard on the wooden windowsills.

A voice. Someone humming. A soft up and down melody, but the words are faint and unclear. Ben's heart races. Pulling himself to the side of the bed, he slips into jeans and a T-shirt and creeps down the hall. He stops at the top of the stairs and looks out the window at Victor's house. The kitchen and living room lights are on. The house was dark when Ben went to bed, though he knew Victor was home. He heard him early in the evening messing around in his backyard. Victor's always messing with something. He's a damn cricket, Ben once told Amy.

Ben starts down the stairs. He stops halfway, listens a second, then heads boldly through the dining room until he reaches the entrance of the living room. There in Ben's favorite chair is a man dressed in black wearing a seaman's coat, collar turned up, precisely as Victor described, precisely as Warren described. The glow of the streetlamp coming through the window is angled onto him like a perfectly placed stage light.

Ben stares at the man.

"Now, now, Ben…come in," the man says. "Don't be shy, my friend. We *are* friends…aren't we?"

Ben's shoulders tighten.

"Here, come here, come in, Ben…take a seat," the man says, pointing to the sofa to his right.

Ben sits on the sofa, the place that fits perfectly with the strategy he laid out.

"It's such a delightful night," the man says in a melodic voice. "There is something about nighttime rain I like. Anyway, I just had to stop by and see how you're doing. And so, that is the question…how *are* you doing?"

"How'd you get in here?" Ben flares.

"Why, the door, of course," The man replies, in a self-evident tone. "Surely you don't think I climbed in a window now, do you?" he says with a chuckle. "Though some people are known to do such things...true? Climb in a window and poke around in someone's basement, let's say. It happens when our curiosity gets the best of us."

"What do you want," Ben growls.

"Oooh, my requests are simple. See, I'm a very honest man. I have no hidden agendas like most people have. No secret plans—"

"And so are mine," Ben says. "You have *two* choices. One, you can get your ass out of here right now, get up and leave. Or two, I'll throw your ass out of here."

The man laughs. "You do have a good sense of humor, Ben. I like that in a person. You've got a lot of gumption...I like that, too."

"What are you doing in Cedar Bluff? And why were you asking my employee about me the other day?"

"So many questions, Ben. So many questions," the man says, lightly, almost jovially. "I'm the one with questions. And indeed, I do have a couple...well, two to be exact. But if it's important to you, I'll answer yours first. Then I'll get to mine." The man sits straight and still, hands across his lap. "What am I doing here in the Bluff? That's what you call it, isn't it? The Bluff. I like that, it's so quaint," he quips, tilting his head a notch. "I'm just passing through, if you really need to know. Originally, I'm from New York. But it makes no difference where I am from. You see, I am Mostredek, sent here by Asmodeus—Asmodeus, the King of Demons—and I have a small proposition to make. The decision will be yours, and somehow I think you already know what I am about to say. Nonetheless, let me explain."

Ben's hands are sweaty; his plan doesn't seem so simple now.

"You have two choices…only two," Mostredek says, holding up a pair of fingers, nails long and pointed. "That's right two choices. You must give me your son, Jimmy, or your wife, Amy. One or the other. If you do that, the deaths in Cedar Bluff, the hangings, will end. There will be no more. If, however, you do *not* comply, I will intercede. There will be swift retribution for you and the killings in Cedar Bluff will continue."

Ben listens intently as he prepares his attack.

"You have forty-eight hours to decide. Exactly forty-eight, not a second longer. And do not think there is a way around this." He holds a hand up and snaps his finger. Flames burn brightly from the tips. He snaps them again and the flames are gone. "Is it clear what I am telling you? Do you understand—"

"You are the devil, and you will never win. *Never!*" Ben's hand moves between the cushions of the sofa. *Where is it? Where?* He searches slowly back and forth. *Fuck…fuck, fuck.* Finally, there at last, his hand lands on it: a black cross, twelve inches long and six across. He pulls it quickly out and holds it toward Mostredek.

Mostredek squeals and reels back.

Standing, Ben waves the cross in front of Mostredek. "*I* am in control, now" he yells. "Yes, *I* am in control and you are helpless. See how you cower, you disgusting creature? *See,*

see?"

Mostredek looks away. Losing strength, he sinks into the chair. His shoulders slope. His head falls to his chest. He tries to move but he is getting weaker by the second. He grinds his jaws and spreads his lips, displaying a set of yellow half-rotted teeth.

Ben's plan is working. He will wait until the man is drained of strength and finish him off. "*Ha*, you never expected this, did you? You, whoever you are, I will destroy you. And then you will rot in hell forever. Forever!"

Mostredek attempts to strike his fingers, trying to draw fire up from hell but nothing happens. In a weak and feeble voice, he mutters, "I will take them. Asmodeus will have them and you cannot stop it."

Ben holds the cross closer. Mostredek cowers farther into the chair. In a last defiant act, he swings his arm and knocks the cross from Ben's hand. It hits the wall behind them and lands below the curtains.

Life begins to flow back into Mostredek. In desperation, Ben grabs him by the neck, throttling him, but in a moment of tremendous strength, Mostredek grasps Ben by the torso. Fingernails dig deep into Ben's flesh. Mostredek lifts Ben like a stuffed animal and hurls him over his shoulder. He lands next to the curtain.

Hunched and bent as though the power of the cross has disfigured him, leaving him weak and lame, Mostredek hobbles toward the door.

All at once, there is a terrible flash of lightning from out-side and a terrible crash of thunder. With it, Mostredek bursts into nothing and vanishes into the warm wet air.

Ben rolls onto his back and sinks into sleep as though tran-quilized.

23

The morning light coming through the window hits Ben in the eye. He climbs slowly to his knees then to his feet, drained of energy. Opening the front door, he is met with fresh sparkling air of the kind that comes after a heavy rain. He remembers everything that happened during the night. He has a feeling that he has succeeded and that the devil has been denied his requests. As he trudges into the kitchen, his cell phone rings. He picks it up from the counter where he left it the night before.

"Hi, hon," Amy says, in a bubbly voice. "Just want to let you know we had a *great* trip. This place, Mankato, is the place for Jimmy all right. He's certain of it now. Oooh my, let me tell you, they have everything he's looking for."

"Ah…that's good," Ben says, as a smile moves across his face.

"We'll be leaving in a short while. It won't take long to get back. Should be there later this afternoon."

Ben goes to work and pours a cup of coffee and pulls a Twinkie from the shelf. He takes a bite and tosses the rest in the trash.

Warren comes in from the bay. He looks at Ben for a second, stops, and says, "Oh, you okay, boss? Don't mean to worry you none now, but you're looking a little peaked today. Everything all right?"

Ben assures him he's fine.

"Saw your bud Victor this morning," Warren says. "He was in here bright and early. Didn't say much...none of that usual Victor pizzazz, the big grin and all. Just nodded toward the back of the car for a tank fill. Paid in cash, too. Oh, now that's something new for Victor. Usually waves that credit card of his out the window like it's a flag at a parade."

Ben explains that Amy and Jimmy are on their way back from Mankato, that they went there to visit the university.

Warren looks out at the sky, blue and bright. "Well, I'm thinking...say, you couldn't pick a better day for a nice drive, huh? Why, almost good enough to get out on the links or something, huh? If I played golf, that is. Never picked up the game though...worried I'd like it too much...oh, ye-uh."

Ben takes a sip of coffee and sets the cup down. Last thing I need now is caffeine, nerves being what they are, he tells himself. He goes out and gasses up a car, works for a couple of hours, and tells Warren he has business at home.

He unrolls the garden hose and waters the front lawn, keeping a close eye of Amy's progress on his phone. She's making good time—all's well. He goes inside and gets out his blood pressure cuff and checks the pressure. Not terrific but not as bad as he expected. Nothing could make him happier now than to see Amy's SUV roll into the drive.

Waiting in the living room, sitting in a chair, the events from the previous night keep flashing through his mind. How will we know we're safe from the devil's curse, he wonders. Everything happened exactly as Victor predicted.

Forty-five slow minutes go by. A Minnesota highway patrol car pulls in the driveway. Ben races to the car. The patrolman gets out. Amy and Jimmy climb from the back seat. Ben learns that Amy's car was T-boned at an intersection just outside Cedar Bluff. The car is totaled but she and Jimmy are fine. Ben's eyes tear up; he lets out a huge sigh of relief.

□

Days pass. Not a peep from Mostredek. No communication, no ultimatums. Ben is convinced he has won the battle with the devil. Ben's spirits gradually improve. He starts to pick up with his routine of spending time in the backyard after dinner, exactly as he has done all summer, exactly but for the absence of Victor now.

24

On Thursday afternoon, Ben cuts his afternoon short and returns home at three-thirty. Warren has the bays under control. One small job, tires and oil.

Ben walks in the house and calls to Amy, doing his best *'Lucy...I'm home'* imitation. He gets no reply. On the kitchen table is a note:

Hi Love. I'm at Victor's. He invited us over, but Jimmy's out with his friends, so I went. Come by when you get home.

Ben knocks on Victor's door. Once, twice, three times. Each, a little harder. The door is unlocked. He opens it and pokes his head inside.

"Hey, it's me. Anyone here?" He steps inside. "Vic, Amy?"

Silence.

He ventures in. Already he has a pretty good idea that Victor has left for good. The dining room table is cleared of his papers—no laptop, no printer. The shades are drawn; the room is stuffy.

Ben walks through the house calling for Amy. The bathroom is empty: no toothpaste, no toothbrush, no assortment of shaving crud, hairbrushes, or soap. The bedroom is bare, too. Just a mattress and an empty chest of drawers. Likewise in the kitchen. A carton of milk in the refrigerator, a lone can of soup in the pantry.

Victor is indeed gone. On the kitchen counter is a note:

Hello Ben. Sorry I missed you. Had to leave rather quickly. But I had a little gift for you and Amy – to thank you for all you did. For all your wonderful Cedar Bluff hospitality. Cheers! Victor.

Calling again, Ben opens the basement door. "Amy…you here?"

He turns on the light and starts down. The thick old basement air falls heavily on him. He stops on the bottom step and looks around. The room hasn't changed much from when he came in through the window. His two skill saws are on the floor where they were before. The rank smell of formaldehyde is still present. Ben's eyes land on the small room Victor constructed in the corner. One thing is notable, however. The hasp is unlocked. The door is open a trace.

Ben walks over. He pulls the door back, a little at first and then more. The room is submerged in darkness. He has a bad feeling that he doesn't like at all. Light seeps in as he gradually opens the door. In front of him is a person standing on a stool, hands in back, duct tape over the mouth, a noose around the neck. A rope is strung taut up to the ceiling.

The person mumbles loudly, trying to call out.

Ben realizes it's Amy. "Don't move! Don't move!" Ben cries. He knows that to slip off the stool would mean certain death. "Stay perfectly still, I'll get you down."

Taking a step into the room, he is pulled back and turned around. Two feet in front of him is Mostredek, decked in black head to toe, looking exactly as he did in Ben's living room.

"Yes, Ben, I have returned," he says, gravely. "I gave you one extra day to decide. Wasn't that nice of me? See, see I *do* have a warm soul. But you didn't decide. I'm *so* disappointed."

Ben lets out a growl and leaps for Mostredek. He grabs him by the throat but is thrown back with a tremendous force, nearly careening onto the stool that holds Amy. Mostredek starts into the room. Ben charges again, this time knocking Mostredek out of the room into the basement. Mostredek gives Ben a ferocious shove, hurling him once more into the room and landing at the foot of the stool. Scrambling to his feet, Ben barrels toward Mostredek.

"Isn't this wonderful," Mostredek says, holding a hand in the air. "Why look at you, you came just in time to watch...to see it all. How perfect!"

Mostredek snaps his fingers, flames dart from the tips.

Ben is immobilized—barely able to pull air into his lungs.

"And now the murders in Cedar Bluff will continue. You see, Ben, you could have stopped them." Mostredek snaps his fingers. The flames go out.

Instantly freed from his rigid stance, Ben leans forward, sucking air into his lungs.

Mostredek moves toward the room.

Ben sees the scraps of wood Victor left behind. Racing over, he picks up a pair of two-by-twos, each roughly ten inches in length. He wheels around and forms a cross and aims it at Mostredek just as he turns toward Ben. Mostredek falls back. His shoulders slump, his head sags, exactly as in Ben's living room.

"You, Mostredek, Asmodeus, whoever the hell you are…you are *finished, finished*," Ben yells.

Mostredek is tipsy. Ben is afraid he will fall back on the stool that supports Amy. He steps toward Mostredek, hoping to lure him out of the room. The ploy is working. Mostredek moves in weak shuffling steps toward Ben; he gasps for air. Unable to hold his hand up, unable to snap his fingers with little more than a lame flick, he falls onto his knees and rolls on his back.

Ben takes the cross and presses it hard on Mostredek's throat. Gurgling, his eyes roll back. It is over.

Ben goes into the room and gently releases Amy from the noose.

25

The next day, gloom as thick as Mississippi River mud fills the Malone household. Amy is shaken to the core. She asks about the person in Victor's basement who put her on the stool and put the noose around her neck, but she doesn't really want to know. She believes it's all somehow linked to Victor; the thought disgusts her.

After many days, Ben eventually returns to work. He tries to be his old self but it's difficult.

Warren comments again about Victor's abrupt departure now almost a week ago. He retells of Victor's demeanor on that morning and how the back seat of the car was jampacked with clothes and things of all sorts.

"I don't know why it is but I'm almost happy the guy's gone," Warren says to Ben yet again. "Maybe I'm too suspicious of outsiders...maybe that's my problem, I suppose, having lived in the Bluff my whole life. People never come here much, do they?" Warren says, looking up from a big truck tire where he's hunting for a nail or a puncture hole. He stops working and stares out the bay. "Oh well, that's sort of how I see it."

Ben says nothing, the memory of him and Mostredek in Victor's basement is all too real. He's hoping that by saving Amy from the devil, the episode is over for good.

Evenings are spent with Ben moping around the house, trying to read the newspaper a little, trying to smile. His desire to sit out back and pop a Summit or a Surly is gone. He's almost afraid that in some surreal way Victor will come strolling casually around the corner. Victor, the last person in the world Ben wants to see right now.

Ben looks out the living room window at the house Victor occupied most of the summer. He imagines Victor still inside, still sitting at the dining room table, still pecking persistently away on the computer keys. Ben stares cholerically at the house; he is filled with disgust. Now, he is certain of what he will do.

Late at night, Ben slips out of bed, gets dressed, sneaks quietly next door, and goes to the basement window. It's still unlocked. He lifts the sash and lowers himself inside. The room is dark but for a thread of light from the moon that feeds its way through the small windows.

Standing still as a cat, he looks around searching for what he's after. He hears something behind him from over by the stairs. Turning quickly, he sees Victor Cartuso on the bottom step.

"Well...*Ben*, my beer-drinking buddy. You have returned. I wondered how long it would take."

Ben's heart pounds.

"Now that you've come back, I'll fill you in on some details. You see...you see, *I* am Mostredek. Yes, that was the deal, the bargain, I made. And indeed, for many years I have been consorting with the devil. He simply made me an offer I couldn't refuse, as the saying goes. The plan was simple. I was to do his bidding and in return I would become very wealthy *and* a very successful author. This is what I wanted all my life. This is all I ever wanted. And indeed, that's precisely what happened. It was almost effortless on my part. Of course, I had to give up a little: my wife, Marla, and yes, even Matthew, my son. Nothing is ever free, is it? Yet, in so doing I made millions of dollars, sold millions of books. Became famous."

Victor moves closer to Ben. Ben steps back, glancing furtively around the room.

"So, according to the deal, I was to become Mostredek and would work for Asmodeus, who has been sentenced to live in Hades forever. I would recruit many more souls into the fold. My job, my task, is to go to small towns like Cedar Bluff and gather as many souls for the devil as possible. I never stay long in these places. It's a nice hiatus from my gorgeous luxury condo in Manhattan. My life has been perfect, you might say, and I have no regrets. This has become my real cause in life...this and my writing." Victor stops talking for a second. He holds his arms out like a preacher in the pulpit, his fingernails long and pointed.

Anger races through Ben. He wants to leap at Victor and beat the crap out of him, but he remembers his previous encounters with Mostredek—his superhuman strength. All the evilness of the devil stored within.

Victor continues, speaking casually as if he's sitting in a chair in Ben's backyard on a hot night holding an ice-cold beer. "You see, we all have a purpose on this planet," he says in a very round and philosophical voice. "A cause, you might say. Yours is to run a pretty good gas station, be a good father and husband. The butcher, the baker, the candlestick maker, they too all have a purpose. Me…well, I am no different, not really. I have been fortunate to succeed in two ways. I am a great and famous author. And I am Mostredek. Aaah, what could be better?"

Ben's eyes search the darkness.

Victor sighs. "Oh, but I do have one last mission before I finally depart from Cedar Bluff." He breathes deeply and exhales. "You, Ben…you will be my last soul. And then I will be gone from this sweet little town forever. So sorry it has come to this, but, well…what can I say." He takes a step toward Ben. "What you will find in the little room I built, the one Amy was in not long ago, what you will find is a rope and a noose and a stool, all fixed to the perfect height for you. It will be fast and painless. Trust me. You may not want to do this, so I will help you." With that, Victor snaps his fingers; flames burn from the tips.

Ben's mind grows foggy. He shakes his head, trying to stay alert. Mounting all his energy, he grabs a ballpeen hammer from the workbench and flings it at Victor. Victor dodges the hammer but in the darkness slips and falls on his side.

With a whack of his foot, Ben kicks over a gallon can of gasoline. Gas splashes across Victor. Fingertips still sporting flames, the gasoline bursts into a wild blaze that engulfs Victor. He calls desperately for help.

Ben grabs the can, opens the top, and douses Victor head to toe and shakes the liquid across the room. The basement is swept in flames.

Ben rushes to the window and is out not a second too soon. He stands and looks momentarily at the inferno in the basement. A terrible odor—the smell of rot and decay, the smell of death—blasts out the window.

Within minutes, Ben is back at home. He falls on the sofa and stares at the ceiling.

26

Four in the morning. Fire trucks pull up at Victor's house. Sirens scream. Lights flash wildly. Flames pour from the windows. Firehoses deliver a torrential storm of water for an hour and half until there is nothing but thin wisps of smoke coming out.

People gather by the street, watching the house turn to blackened embers. Ben stands next to Ralph Morgenstern, a senior fireman. "So, what do you think it was?" Ben asks, nodding at the house.

"Can't say just yet," Morgenstern replies. "Looks to have started in the basement...seems so." He shrugs. "Could even be arson, I guess."

Ben nods again, hands in his pockets.

"Is this the place that writer fella lived? The one Warren told me about a while back?"

"It's the place," Ben says. "He left though...left a week or so ago. Not sure where, exactly. New York, maybe. Gone, that's all I know."

"Sorta an odd fella. That's what I heard," Morgenstern says.

"Whew," Ben mumbles. "Could say that again."

www.ingramcontent.com/pod-product-compliance
Lightning Source LLC
Chambersburg PA
CBHW021202110726
47900CB00002B/691